Blood Brother
Roy   hilip,
YA   : Roy
Gra   Valley

D1170297

Blood Brothers
in Louisbourg

by Philip Roy

GRAND VALLEY PUBLIC LIBRARY

For Don

Copyright © 2012 Philip Roy

This book is a work of fiction. The characters and events depicted are products of the author's imagination.

All rights reserved. No part of this work may be reproduced or used in any form or by any means, electronic or mechanical, including photocopying, recording or any information storage or retrieval system, without the prior written permission of the publisher. Cape Breton University Press recognizes fair dealing exceptions under Access Copyright. Responsibility for the opinions, research and the permissions obtained for this publication rest with the author.

Cape Breton University Press recognizes the support of the Canada Council for the Arts, Block Grant program, and the Province of Nova Scotia, through the Department of Communities, Culture and Heritage, for our publishing program. We are pleased to work in partnership with these bodies to develop and promote our cultural resources.

Cover design by Cathy MacLean Design, Pleasant Bay, NS
Layout by Mike Hunter, Port Hawkesbury and Sydney, NS.
First printed in Canada

Library and Archives Canada Cataloguing in Publication

Roy, Philip, 1960-
Blood brothers in Louisbourg : a novel / Philip Roy.
ISBN 978-1-897009-72-7
I. Title.
PS8635.O91144B56 2012   C813'.6   C2012-903185-2

Cape Breton University Press
P.O. Box 5300
Sydney, Nova Scotia B1P 6L2 CA
www.cbupress.ca

Blood Brothers in Louisbourg

by Philip Roy

Cape Breton University Press
Sydney, Nova Scotia, Canada

I met a ghost once. Well, he wasn't really a ghost, he was a warrior who could fly over walls like a bird and run under the ground like a rat and never make a sound. I saw him only a dozen times or so when he didn't even know I was there. We never spoke. I suppose he did try to kill me. He thought I was his enemy. I admired him anyway.

Chapter One

My father served the King, Louis XV. He was a captain and military engineer in the *Compagnies franches de la Marine*. He sailed on the King's ships and wore the King's uniform and liked to joke that he sat on the King's pot. But he never actually met the King. He built His fortresses, carried His pistol and wore His insignia close to his heart but never once set eyes upon Him. I couldn't understand how he could be so devoted to a person he'd never met.

One day in my fifteenth year my father had me accompany him in his carriage to Paris, where he would receive new orders. It was a snowy day; the horses were slipping on the road. My father was in a good mood. The King had just declared war on the English. This, he said, was great news. The King would almost certainly send him back to the great Fortress of Louisbourg, where the fortifications, which he had helped design and build, would need reinforcing.

"And if I go, Jacques, then you will come with me."

I thought he was joking. But he wasn't.

"What would *I* do there?"

"Wear a uniform, carry a musket and defend the King! At Louisbourg, Jacques, you will become a man."

I stared out the carriage window. The wind spun the snow into spirals. I was not close to my father. He was a stranger when I was growing up because he was always away. My earliest memory of him was when my mother put me on his knee and he picked me up, shook me and laughed. He smelled strange. He sounded strange. I was frightened and I cried. He was never home for more than a few months at a time and never paid much attention to me when he was. Now, suddenly, he was taking an interest in me.

My father loved uniforms, weapons, military strategy and anything to do with killing the enemy efficiently. He spoke of the efficiency of killing soldiers the same way he spoke of the efficiency of bridges, roads or fortifications. He loved building things and he loved war. He said the greatest glory a man could achieve was to distinguish himself in battle, especially to die in battle.

I really didn't understand. I understood his fascination with building things, such as roads and bridges and walls, but where was the glory in killing people? Or dying? That didn't make any sense to me at all. I loved learning about new things, especially scientific inventions such as the diving bell, the steam engine and the pianoforte, and music and books. Weapons were interesting too – how they were constructed and how they worked – but it bothered me that they were used to kill people. When I was little, I saw a man crushed beneath a carriage. He fell down in the street and the wheels rolled over him and killed him. I learned then that the body was not made to stand up to wood and metal. Even the strongest man's body could be broken with a block of wood. When I thought of people creating mechanical inventions to rip apart the flesh and bones of other people, I felt horrified inside. But that was a secret I kept to myself. I didn't want anyone to think I was afraid.

At fifteen I had already exceeded my father's expectations for education. No one needed *that* much book learning, he said. Now was the time to concentrate on the manly arts: swordsmanship, wrestling and musketry. I shut my eyes when he said that. I *hated* wrestling, was hopeless with a sword and couldn't fire a musket to save my life. Other boys my age had fathers or older brothers around to show them those things. I didn't. Not to worry, said my father. There was still time to learn. At Louisbourg I would learn everything I needed to know to become a man. As the carriage entered the city gates I made an attempt to discuss Voltaire, my favourite writer, in the hope of showing my father that my talents lay elsewhere. Voltaire was a visionary. He wanted to make things better for France, not just for the King. The future was in the brandishing of new ideas, not swords and muskets. "Voltaire has a new way of …"

"Voltaire?! Voltaire is a criminal!" my father shouted. "That is why he was thrown in the Bastille. He wrote against the King. He should have been shot for that! No, you need to study the manly arts now, Jacques. You have read enough books."

I felt desperate. "Will I be able to bring my violoncello?"

He smiled, but it wasn't genuine. "Sure. Why not? Bring anything you like, though I doubt you will feel much like playing it there. The Fortress of Louisbourg is the greatest defence system in the New World, Jacques. Just wait until you see it. You will be so impressed. And with all our military preparations, I think you will find little time for music."

As the snow thickened on the branches outside, I tried to imagine raising a heavy musket to my shoulder, aiming and firing at an enemy soldier. He would have a look of horror on his face. He would fall to his knees, drop forward onto the ground and his blood would drip into the soil. Then, someone else would shoot me and I would fall. I would bleed to death too. I hadn't even reached my sixteenth birthday. Would my father see glory in that? That was insane. War was insane. All the great philosophers had said so. But my father hadn't read them.

As for the New World, why should I care about a place so far away? Wasn't it just filled with savages? I wouldn't go. And if my father forced me to, I would hate him forever.

———

My mother was upset at the thought of losing me, but would not go against my father's wishes. I could see it in her eyes, behind her tears. I didn't blame her for that. That was the way of our society. We sat down for tea the next morning. "I will bring my violoncello, Mama," I said.

She looked troubled.

"What? What is it?"

"Jacques, your father has decided your violoncello will stay behind."

"No, no. He clearly said I could bring it."

She shook her head. "I don't think he meant it."

My mind raced. I thought of running away. I had cousins in Provence. But they would not take me in if I went against my father's will. "Are you sure, Mama? He clearly said I could take whatever I liked."

"I believe he will tell you there is space for one chest only. Can you fit your violoncello in one chest?"

"Perhaps, if I remove the neck and bridge. And I pack my things around it."

"Jacques …" She took my hands. "Your father has it firmly in his mind that you will come back from the New World a grown man. That you will join him in the *Compagnies franches de la Marine*."

"And build fortresses?"

"Yes."

I shook my head. "Mama, I will write to you every day and make certain the letters are sent with each sailing ship."

My mother's tears fell hard. How I hated to see her cry. "I know, my son. I will write you as well." She forced herself to smile. "And perhaps you will find the pendant I gave to your father on his first voyage there. It is a turquoise oval cut with a woman's face. Look, it matches this ring. See how lovely it is? My grandmother gave it to me when I was a little girl. It was my favourite possession."

"If it is there, Mama, I will find it."

—

I packed my violoncello. I took it secretly to the instrument maker's where they separated the neck from the body and gave me glue for reattaching it. I wrapped my clothes around it and just managed to squeeze the body inside the chest. I wrapped the neck, bridge and bow, rolled up the strings and packed them all separately. This left little space for anything else so I chose my books carefully and took only what clothing I couldn't live without. I was hardly expecting to frequent high society in the rustic Fortress of Louisbourg.

Chapter Two

Two-feathers woke in freshly fallen snow. He raised the spruce boughs that had kept him warm and listened to the silence. He had been woken by the squeal of a rabbit caught in a snare he had set the night before. Moving quietly through the snow, he grabbed the animal, freed it from the snare and held it firmly against his stomach. Petting its soft ears and whispering words of apology and gratitude, he deftly slit its throat and held on as it released its life to him.

In the pit where he had slept he built a fire, skinned the rabbit and sat roasting it. The wind twisted softly through the trees carrying the earliest scent of spring. Two-feathers breathed deeply and smiled. He had survived the harshest winter. He was not so far from the sea now, where the bluecoats had constructed their great village. It was legendary among his people, a village that had consumed the forest for half a day's walk in every direction, with weapons that blew stones the weight of a man out to sea, and a harbour of giant canoes that carried warriors beyond the sea and sky. Two-feathers was keen to see it all for himself, though that was not why he had come.

He tied his deerskin clothes tightly at the wrists and ankles to trap his body's heat, picked up his bow and pack and followed the frozen river. Soon the rivers would break apart and flow freely to the sea, and they would run thick with salmon. In the shadows of morning he heard the snap of a branch and turned – there, at the river's edge, a young doe was drinking; one he had seen the day before. She dropped her head in solitude; she did not know he was there. Two-feathers quickly fitted an arrow to his bow. The shot was clear, but he hesitated. He could not take the life of a deer for just one meal. Pursing his lips he whistled, and the startled deer fled like the wind. In its escape it roused a partridge. Two-feathers quickly aimed, and the bird gave itself in the doe's place.

As he hung the partridge from his pack, he wondered if the doe had come as a sign from the spirit of his mother, Running-deer. Perhaps she had come to guide him, or warn him, or maybe even to apologize for having left him. Many years before, he was told by his chief, she had travelled with a trading party to the blue-coats' village, where she fell in love with a young bluecoat warrior. The bluecoats sometimes took wives from his people for companionship as well as for advantage in the fur trade. But the young warrior who had won Running-deer's affection did not want to keep her; after two seasons he returned to his own land, and she to her people, the Mi'kmaq, where she gave birth to Two-feathers, so named because the blood of two peoples flowed through his veins.

Three years later, Running-deer left once more to try to re-unite with Two-feathers' father, who had returned but was now married in his own land. Despairingly, she threw herself at a man who had closed his heart and would not see her. Alone and dis-traught, she ran from the fortress in the dead of winter. That was the story as Two-feathers had received it. No one knew what had happened to her after that, whether she met with wild animals, succumbed to the cold or simply died of a broken heart. She was never seen again.

Two-feathers was raised by the Mi'kmaq. He became the brightest young warrior of his tribe. The role of warrior came to him as naturally as flight to a bird, and he loved it with every part of his being. And yet, even as a boy he sensed that, since his father could not be counted among the Mi'kmaq, it was even more important that he become stronger, faster, more skilled and more aware than his companions. And he did. He excelled in hunting, fishing, scouting and trapping. He could make fires when the rain would not end and keep warm in the deepest cold. Still, he was never able to forget that his father was not one of them. He liked to believe that his father was a noble warrior among his *own* people, but a nagging doubt haunted him. What noble warrior would put the mother of his child out in the cold? Now, almost a man himself, Two-feathers needed to find out.

———

The woods were full of spirits. Two-feathers felt them around him in the day and night. Sometimes they took the form of animals, their favourite, and sometimes trees or plants. Usually they were peaceful and helpful, but occasionally they were angry and he had to be careful when crossing a river, or climbing a rock face or hunting a bear. This he had learned the hard way, having once brought down a young bear with his bow and arrow. As he approached, the bear suddenly leapt to its feet and clawed at his leg, cutting a deep wound. Two-feathers retaliated by stabbing the bear with his knife until it was dead. Now he carried a scar that reminded him that the spirits kept their own council and could change their minds without warning.

The woods were also frequented by trappers and soldiers: bluecoats, who were friendly; and redcoats, who were not. Two-feathers came upon parties of each but went out of his way to avoid them. They were strong, capable men, these white-skinned warriors, but they carried strange and dangerous sickness. They salted their food until it tasted like seawater, and drank a poisonous drink that made them laugh, sing and dance until they fell down, but clouded their senses so that they could not shoot straight, nor walk straight, nor even stand up if they drank too much of it. To the Mi'kmaq this poison was particularly dangerous. Two-feathers was told many times by his chief and the warriors who trained him that he must never drink it or, once he started, he would never be able to stop. And then, though he would laugh, sing and dance, his arrows would no longer hit their targets and he would wake in the morning with pain and thunder in his head. And so he promised himself, as he promised his elders, that he would never drink the poison of the pale-skinned warriors from a faraway land, even though his father was one of them.

He could always smell, hear and see the soldiers long before they would know he was there. They travelled noisily and heavily, wrapped in so many furs they could not run nor even walk quickly through the deep snow. They stopped often and ate for three men each. But he did like their music, which they played at night when they made camp. He would sometimes camp not far away just to listen, though they would not know he was there.

Two-feathers' greatest skill was moving through the woods with invisibility. This he had learned from his teachers, but also from the animal spirits. To carry invisibility you had to first believe that you were. Then, you could cross the snow-covered river leaving no tracks because you had no weight. You could pass through the woods in silence because you made no sound. You could slip between trees unseen because you had no shape and cast no shadow. Only then, when you felt this way, could you move amongst strangers without them seeing you.

In the afternoon he heard them – soldiers – passing through the woods with a noise like falling trees. Turning into the wind, he closed his eyes and raised his nose. Their scent was strong. There were at least half a dozen of them. He wondered why they had come so far inland where there were no trading parties and few furs. And then he saw them. Redcoats! But this was land held by the bluecoats, with the help of the Mi'kmaq. Why would a party of redcoats travel so far north? Was this a scouting party? Were the redcoats preparing an attack? Two-feathers didn't care for either group of warriors, but since his people were allied with the bluecoats he felt a responsibility to find out why the redcoats were here. And so he followed them. As it turned out, they were headed in the same direction – towards the bluecoats' great village.

Chapter Three

We sailed from St. Malo in the northwest, on the 27th of March. Ships from St. Malo sailed all over the world. It was a three-day journey by coach to get there. I travelled alone; my father followed later with his regiment. That was a good thing. Three days in a stuffy coach was bad enough, but if I had to listen to him rage against the English all the way I would have gone insane. He would have supported a war against the Austrians or the Persians or the Mongolians, if the King had declared one. War was war to a man who believed in war. However, opinions about the war actually varied quite a bit in France as I learned during the coach ride.

It was crowded. I ended up giving my window seat to a young lady travelling with her mother. Now I was boxed in and couldn't see much out the window. And so I buried my head in my book. It was a copy of Voltaire's *English Essays*, in which he praises the English parliamentary system and criticizes the French monarchy. This was the book that had been banned in France, and the reason Voltaire had been imprisoned in the Bastille. Even so, there were copies being quietly handed around and I had borrowed one from an English friend of mine who played violin. Voltaire really cared about France and its people. You could tell by the way he wrote. Yes, his ideas were revolutionary, but that's what was so exciting. Real change would take courage. And Voltaire was courageous. Even the King had been unable to shut him up. As I stared out through the little patch of window, I thought how much more noble it would be to die for a revolutionary idea than for a senseless war.

As I slowly read and re-read pages of the book, which wasn't easy with the coach swaying and bouncing along the road, a rather angry-looking man across from me was watching. He wasn't really paying attention. He was sleepy. He did not strike me as an educated man, but after an hour or so his gaze slowly slid across the cover of my book. I watched as his eyes suddenly opened wide, and a look of disgust appeared on his face.

"Hey!" he barked. "What rubbish is this?"

He jumped to his feet. All in one motion he grabbed the book out of my hands, leaned across the lap of the young lady without excusing himself, opened the window and threw the book out. He sat back down with such an angry expression I didn't dare say a word.

"Heretic!" he yelled at me.

The next thing that happened surprised me even more. The man to my right, a well-dressed, elderly man, raised his cane and bumped against the roof of the coach, ordering the riders to stop. The coach came to a halt with lots of noise and shaking of the horses. The older man stepped out and held the door. Very politely he said to me, "Go. Fetch your book."

"No!" screamed the other man. "I will not ride in a coach with a heretic!"

I saw him reach clumsily for the hilt of his sword, but the elderly man drew his own sword so quickly it appeared as if by magic. He bowed and apologized to the ladies, then politely said, "If Monsieur feels so strongly, perhaps he would like to take a moment to step outside the coach."

The angry man took his hand away from the hilt of his sword and looked away, mumbling under his breath.

"My young scholar," the older man said to me, "fetch your book."

Excusing myself, I hopped out of the coach, ran down the road and found my book. I wiped the mud off it, straightened up its cover and put it into my pocket. Then I returned to the coach, thanked the elderly man and took my seat. As we resumed our journey, the man opposite me sat burning up with rage. If ever a man could have exploded out of anger it would have been him. At the next exchange of horses he left the coach and stayed behind to wait for another. He said he would not ride with heretics and trai- tors and swore that we were all damned to burn in Hell. I found it amazing that a single book could stir up so much anger, especially when the offended man had probably never even read it.

At St. Malo the ship sat in the harbour like a floating bee's nest. Sailors climbed all over it, loading it and preparing it for sea. At first glance I shook my head. Something about it didn't look seaworthy to me, even though I didn't know anything about sail- ing and had never even been on a boat before. There was nothing quick-looking about it; it just looked heavy, stumpy and slow. For two days they continued loading it until I thought it was going to sink. I smiled when they picked up my chest and carried it on board.

Finally, my father boarded the ship with his regiment and all were given sleeping quarters below deck. As I watched the sol- diers march on board I thought the ship would sink for sure. Then I began to realize that there was a relationship between wood and water that was beyond all manner of reason. A ship was to a sailor what a donkey was to a farmer – a beast of burden.

I had to confess there was a moment, just a brief moment, when we first came under sail – when the ship cleared the harbour and caught its first gust of wind with full sails – when I felt a tinge of excitement. I felt the pull of the ship beneath my feet. I turned and looked at my father. He was as excited as a child.

"How now, Jacques?" he yelled.

I smiled a little. I couldn't help it. A few hours later we were barely out of sight of land when I fell into the worst case of seasick- ness anyone ever had. Thus began the worst month of my entire life. I felt so sick with the movement of the sea that I truly wanted to die. Night and day I lay on my bunk, except when my father forced me to my feet and onto the deck for fresh air. I wanted to die, just die and put an end to the terrible sickness in my head and stomach.

But I didn't die. Neither did I improve. At first my father was understanding. He laughed and said, "The sea will do you good. Give you the stomach of a man." But after a week or so of my lying around whimpering like a dog, I think he began to feel embarrassed for me. "Come on, Jacques! Pull yourself together. Find the man inside of yourself!"

I didn't care. I didn't care about his stupid fortress or stupid war or stupid ideas of what a man was supposed to be, I just wanted to get off that cursed, floating nightmare. Halfway across the Atlantic, which I was beginning to believe stretched on forever and ever, and just when I thought things could never get worse … they did.

I had soiled my clothes with sickness and my father went looking through my chest to find more. I never knew he was looking. He found the chest. Then, he found the violoncello. Filled with frustration and shame on my account, he broke into a rage when he saw the instrument taking up so much space, space that might have been filled with the muskets, pistols and swords of a "real" man going to war. He never said a word to me, just passed by with the body of the violoncello in one hand, the neck and bow in the other. I clambered out of bed after him. By the time I reached the deck he was already at the stern of the ship. I had hardly eaten in weeks, and my legs were wobbly. I made a desperate attempt to catch him, to yell at him to stop, but I was too late. Raising the violoncello above his head, he threw it overboard into the sea. The wind howled like a demon as the violoncello disappeared beneath the waves without a sound.

We didn't talk anymore after that. He occasionally barked a few orders at me and I obeyed, but I never looked at him or answered. I was fully prepared to suffer a whipping if he insisted on giving me one, and I think he realized that. Perhaps he felt he had gone too far. I never knew. My seasickness cleared up shortly afterwards. Something changed inside of me too, though I didn't know what it was. My father, no doubt, must have thought it was a change towards manhood. But that was the last time we ever made direct eye contact.

Well … there would be one more time.

Chapter Four

The redcoat stood on the ice and raised his musket. The deer turned her head with concern. She sensed his presence but was hearing sound from all directions and was confused. For two days the temperature had risen above freezing and the woods were filled with the anticipation of spring. The soldier braced himself and took careful aim. How pleased he would be to provide fresh meat for his companions. He placed his finger on the trigger and made one final guess for the wind.

At that very moment, Two-feathers let his arrow fly. The arrow sliced through the air and struck the bough directly above the deer. She bolted. The soldier followed her with his eye and pulled the trigger. The musket fired with a sharp concussion that echoed through the woods but missed its target. The noise angered the river. It opened up the ice directly beneath the soldier and swallowed him, musket and all. Two-feathers watched as the redcoat slipped beneath the ice without a trace. It happened too quickly and he was too far away to try to save him. The ice straightened itself and there was nothing left but the redcoat's tracks in the snow.

Two-feathers waited until the other redcoats came looking for their hunter. He saw them follow his tracks onto the river and wondered how many more the angry spirit would take. There were only five of them left. When they reached the end of their companion's tracks the river opened again and grabbed at two of them, but the others held on and fought for them. As they fought bravely, the angry spirit let them go.

The redcoats returned to their camp shouting and shaking their heads. They were angry with the river spirit and afraid of it. Perhaps they would not go any further now. But Two-feathers would. It was the third time he had rescued the young doe and now he knew she was definitely following him, or perhaps leading him. Now that she had crossed the frozen river, he would also.

As twilight descended and the redcoats drowned their sorrow in poisonous drink, Two-feathers went to the river's edge and asked for safe crossing. The river spirit refused. He explained that he needed to cross the river in order to follow the spirit of his mother, who had taken the form of a deer. The river spirit was silent. It was considering his request. Suddenly a wind gusted from behind and pushed him forwards. Two-feathers took this as a sign of permission. Standing tall, he walked boldly across the ice. He knew it was important to show that he was not afraid. If the river spirit detected any weakness in his courage it would swallow him instantly.

On the other side he did not see the doe but found her tracks. That was enough. He was certain she would appear to him again.

He found a gully, cut spruce boughs for his bed, made a fire and roasted a rabbit. The meat was tender and filling, yet not completely satisfying. Always in the spring he felt a hunger for the fruits of summer, the cranberries, blackberries, blueberries, apples, tubers and chestnuts. In the winter he ate like a fox, feasting on rabbits, pigeons and partridge. In the summer he ate like a bear, scooping salmon from the river and berries from the fields. Winter was a time of survival. Summer was a time of replenishing. Only the summertime provided the nourishment he needed to stay healthy and strong.

Two-feathers lay down in his bed and pulled the boughs around him. He drifted off to sleep dreaming of the young doe standing in a field of cranberries. In his dream, she spoke to him, with the voice of his mother.

"I have come to you," she said, "to give your heart rest. I want you to know that, though I died young, I am content where I am. I am happy. You must not worry for me."

The dream was pleasant and comforting but not the only visitation he received that night. Some time later, in the dead of night, he heard the howl of a wolf. But this was not a dream. It was a rare sound in the woods. Ever since the coming of warriors from beyond the sea, the wolf was rarely heard and almost never seen. And yet, Two-feathers recognized the howl instantly. He had no doubt it was an angry spirit coming to frighten him, to make him turn back. As he lay still and listened to the howls growing closer, he had to fight down his fear. He was no match against a full-grown wolf, especially in the dark. How he wished he had kept the fire going and had gathered more wood. If he kept a roaring fire through the night he might have held the wolf off from attacking until morning. But it was too late now.

The wolf's howl was very close. Of all the sounds that haunted the woods, it was the most frightening. It was a sound that spread hopelessness and fear. Two-feathers felt a shiver go up his spine. He scarcely breathed. Then, he heard the punch of paws in the snow. They were so heavy. The wolf had found his sleeping berth. Next came the sound of violent breathing as the beast sniffed at his spruce-bough cocoon. And then ... the growl. It was low and deep and terrifying, designed to scare the courage out of every living creature.

But Two-feathers was a warrior. If he were going to die, he would die a warrior, not a coward. Responding to the wolf's intimidation, he raised a growl from within his own chest. He didn't even hear it himself, so consumed was he with setting loose a growl more vicious than the wolf's own. Two-feathers' growl told the wolf that he was a great warrior about to rise from his sleep and take his long knife and strike the wolf down and slay him and skin him and wear his fur and dangle his teeth in a chain of decoration. All of this Two-feathers communicated in a single growl, with the greatest conviction of his life.

And he really would have risen out of his bed and struck at the wolf with all his skill. And likely he would have died. But he was never given the chance to find out. The wolf was satisfied that Two-feathers was a worthy opponent. There was no need to spill blood to prove anything. And the thought of its teeth dangling in a neckpiece did not especially appeal to the beast. There were many delicious creatures in the woods that would not be nearly so much trouble to catch and eat. So the wolf snorted and moved on. Two-feathers breathed deeply and tried to relax. The creation of such a powerful growl had exhausted him and caused his body to break out in a sweat. He shivered for a long time until his limbs finally dried and warmed again and he was able to fall back to sleep.

In the morning the doe appeared once again. Two-feathers was glad to see that she had also escaped the hunger of the wolf. But something in the look of her was different. It was as if she carried an impatience, as if where she was leading him was now not so far away. Was this, he wondered, why the spirit of the wolf had visited him; to scare him away from what he would discover today?

He followed the doe through the morning, catching glimpses of her twice and staying steadily on her tracks until they came to a great oak, an enormous tree of many generations' growth. Such a tree would surely be visited by rich and benevolent spirits. Two-feathers stood and admired the tree for a long time, offering words of respect. In its branches the voices of birds sang the song of spring, while below on the ground the ice and snow had melted away from its great trunk, revealing yellowed grass with a hint of green. Two-feathers was in awe. It was as if he had discovered the very origin of spring.

A closer look at the tree revealed an opening on one side. The trunk contained a cavity large enough for a small person to crawl inside. Gripping the wet bark with both hands, he stuck his head in. His heart beat wildly. He knew he had come to a sacred place. After a moment's adjustment to the darkness inside the tree, he opened his eyes and stared. There, curled up like an infant, was his beloved mother.

Chapter Five

On the third of May, 1744, we sailed into Louisbourg Harbour. If this was spring in the New World I wasn't very impressed. It was cold and damp, and I couldn't see anything but rocks and a few stubby bushes. There wasn't a single flower to be seen, or even a tree. There were tree stumps but no trees. There were many cannon pointed in our direction as we glided into the harbour. Several were fired to announce our arrival. It was a wonder they didn't sink us right then and there. I had only one thought in my head – to get off that cursed ship and never set foot upon one again. That left me with a problem, of course – how to return to France. For the time being, I decided not to think about it.

The soldiers on the ship were shouting, and the people on the quay were yelling, groping at the air and waving their arms. We dropped anchor, lowered our rowboats and rowed to shore. I saw when we got closer that the people were not yelling out of excitement as much as desperation. They were more interested in the food and supplies we were carrying than the pleasure of our company.

I followed my father onto the quay. We were met by the Governor of Louisbourg, no less, and a few other local dignitaries, who stood out from the people like flowers amongst weeds. The Governor, in particular, looked out of place. He carried himself with an air of exasperation or illness, as if his being here was by accident. The people around him were very rough – soldiers and fishermen mostly. Their children were worse. They were straggly and unkempt. Not a single person struck me as having the strength, the will, nor the ferocity to defend the fortress against the English. They looked already defeated.

We were introduced to the Governor briefly; then to Monsieur Anglaise, a rich merchant who was staying with the Governor; then to the Master Engineer – a man my father liked a lot; and to the fortress priest – a man my father appeared to hate. I found the priest rather grim myself, but everyone seemed rather grim. I didn't realize that they were practically starving. The arrival of our ship was their salvation.

I was given a bed in a barracks – my father insisted; he wanted me to experience the soldier's life – but he stayed at the Master Engineer's house across the street. I could tell from the way engineers were treated that they were held in high regard in Louisbourg. They were the creators of the fortress's impenetrable defence system. I didn't see what was so impenetrable about it; the walls were just heavy blocks of stone. And the stone looked soft, as if it would crumble if you hit it hard enough.

The Governor lived in his own residence above the town. It was surrounded by a wall and moat. Entrance to his courtyard was gained through one gate only, across a drawbridge guarded by soldiers. No one passed through the gate without the Governor's official consent, but it was the guards who decided who would receive the Governor's consent and who wouldn't.

After a few days of settling in, during which time I never even saw my father, so busy was he preparing to refortify the fortress, I was called to the Governor's residence. A young servant, just a boy, came into the barracks first thing in the morning and shook my shoulder gently. I couldn't imagine why the Governor would want to see me.

As I left my bed and followed the boy through the cobblestone streets I realized that the supplies of our ship had already raised the spirits of the people. I saw it on their faces in the street. Gone was the dull greyness. In its place were rosy cheeks, laughter and a skip in their step. We had also brought news of war. This raised the spirits of many too. I couldn't imagine why.

The guards on the drawbridge knew I was coming and let me pass. I think they shared a joke on my account because I didn't look anything like a soldier. I didn't care. I wasn't trying to impress anyone here, least of all the soldiers.

The first door inside the Governor's courtyard led into the fortress chapel, where I caught a glimpse of the priest, who did not appear to have cheered up at all. We continued on our way until I was led into the rooms of the Governor, where I stood and waited. But it wasn't the Governor who wanted to see me at all. It was the rich merchant, Monsieur Anglaise. He got up from a chair next to the Governor and greeted me warmly. He seemed very happy to see me. I had no idea why.

"Ahhhhh ... Master Jacques! At last. Please come in. You have met the Governor."

He gestured towards the Governor. The Governor nodded and raised his hand frivolously but never said a word. I bowed deeply. "It has been my honour, sir."

M. Anglaise gestured for me to sit on a plush velvet chair in a corner of the room. Tea was brought in by a young maid and laid on an ornate serving table. I was impressed with the elegant décor of the room. It was as if a small piece of proper French society had been transported into the wilds of the New World.

M. Anglaise was surprisingly talkative and appeared to have the answers to all of his questions before he even asked them. "Jacques. I understand you are an educated young man."

I shrugged my shoulders. "I have read a few books, sir."

"That is the answer of an educated man. Have you read Voltaire?"

"Yes, sir."

"Good! Then you know that there is at least one man in France who can tell the difference between a king and an opulent ass."

I started to smile then bit my lip. He changed his expression suddenly and stared at me intensely, not in an unfriendly way. "Words spoken in this room do not leave this room. Do you understand?"

"Yes, sir."

"Good. Have you read Michel de Montaigne?"

"Yes, sir. Some."

"Good. Plato?"

"Yes, sir. The dialogues."

"And *The Republic*?"

"Not yet. I'm planning to."

"Ahhh, yes, you must! Then you will really understand where Voltaire is coming from."

"Yes, sir."

"A monarchy is an extravagant thing, Jacques. It's too costly for any country. Plato understood that two thousand years ago."

"Yes, sir."

I glanced at the Governor. I wondered what he thought of M. Anglaise calling the King an ass. It was probably treason, or blasphemy, punishable by death. But the Governor didn't appear to be paying attention. He started coughing. M. Anglaise got up from his seat, crossed the room, put his hand on the Governor's shoulder and squeezed it. Then he pulled it away and paced about the room thoughtfully. "Tell me, Jacques. Have you ever managed to read Boethius?"

"*The Consolation of Philosophy*. Yes, sir."

"Ah, you are well educated indeed. How peculiar to have been raised in the home of a military engineer. I take it you don't share your father's views on war?"

"No, sir. I believe the destiny of France lies in the spread of new ideas, not weapons."

"Indeed! A delightfully revolutionary view. Be careful you don't find yourself in a dungeon, my passionate young scholar. You must know that Boethius bestowed his philosophy upon us from the confines of a dungeon, do you?"

"No, sir, I didn't know that."

"Yes, indeed. He fell out of favour with the ruling elite. Do you understand the function of a dungeon, Jacques?"

"To punish, sir?"

"Not merely, Jacques. Not merely. The function of a dungeon is to destroy the spirit of a man. Our engineers are proud of their dungeons. They claim they are escape-proof."

M. Anglaise stopped pacing and stared out the window. He seemed far away. "But I don't imagine we have a Boethius in our dungeon now."

"No, sir. Is there anyone in the dungeon, sir?"

M. Anglaise raised his eyebrows and deferred the question to the Governor. The Governor wiped his mouth with his handkerchief and answered dryly. "What? Oh. Yes. Yes, of course. A few drunks, I think."

M. Anglaise looked out the window again. I still didn't know why he had summoned me. "Tell me, Jacques. Do you subscribe to the notion of the 'noble savage'?"

"I don't know, sir. I have read about it. Having never seen one, I don't know what to think."

"It is a romantic notion, but there must be something to it. All our great writers have written of it. I am afraid we are a poor influence on the Natives here, Jacques. They still trust us though we steal their land and kill them with disease. Certainly, if there are noble people in the New World it is not the French."

He turned from the window and faced me again. "The reason I have asked you here, Jacques, is that I have a daughter. She is a delicate and intelligent creature, the treasure of my heart. Celestine is her name. She is almost sixteen, and, like you, comes from good society and is well educated. Her mother died three years ago. It was a loss from which she has not recovered. I was unwilling to leave her behind, and, against my better judgment, brought her here, where I believe she is unhappy. Well ... I *know* she is unhappy. I understand that you are accomplished in the playing of the violoncello, is this true?"

"It is my passion, sir."

"Excellent! Celestine enjoys the violoncello more than anything else. I do not know if she has any talent; she has not benefited from expert teaching and I am tone deaf. If you would be willing to commit some of your time and energy to her musical education, thereby bringing a few rays of sunshine into her dreary existence, I would be most grateful and will, in return, compensate you during your stay here in any way that I can."

"I would be honoured, sir."

"Splendid! That is what I hoped you would say. You will find her in the sitting room upstairs. Please don't be put off by her dour disposition and reticence. She has a cheery heart, really, and a sharp wit too if you can coax it out of her. It has not been an easy thing for her to spend so much time amongst the likes of soldiers and fishermen."

"I will do my best, sir."

He smiled, nodded his head and turned his back to me. I took that as a sign to leave. I bowed respectfully and left the room.

I climbed the stairs and stood at the doorway to the upper sitting room. It was just as fancy as downstairs. A maid stood in my way, told me to wait, then came back and led me into the room.

As I entered, I saw a shy but pretty girl turn from her writing desk and look up. She said a word or two to the maid and, like a lady, held out her hand to me. I crossed the room, took it and lightly kissed it. She had the look of someone who had been ill, though her cheeks were rosy. Probably they were coloured with powder. Her dress, ribbons, jewellery and shoes were all the latest fashion in France and were quite elegant. The fragrance of her perfume made me think of flowers. We could have been in any drawing room in Paris, in any capital of Europe really, anywhere but in the New World.

As a well-trained young lady she looked directly into my eyes and made an effort to smile. But it wasn't very convincing. Her lips curled up but the corners of her mouth stayed down as if they were weighted with bags of salt. Her eyes looked tired and wounded. The wound was deep. I bowed my head. "I am honoured to meet you, Mademoiselle."

Chapter Six

The bones lay curled up like an infant beneath her deerskin clothing. The skin was gone but hair still graced the skull like soft brown autumn grass. The bones of her feet disappeared inside rabbit-fur moccasins. She had crawled in on a winter's day.

Two-feathers stared for a very long time. The sacred tree was a very fitting resting place for his mother; he was not upset to have found her so. And yet, the certainty that she had gone into the spirit world opened a fresh wound in his heart for which there was no medicine. The only weapon against such pain was acceptance. But it did not sit as well as it might have. Half of his quest still lay unsolved.

He took his time and prepared a comfortable camp where he would stay for a few days. He wanted to say many prayers in honour of his mother. And so he cut the stems of young poplar trees, peeled wide sheets of bark from old birch trees and fashioned a small teepee. In front of it he dug a pit and rounded it with stones. There he lit a fire that he kept going for three days. He searched the melting woods for the roots of plants, which he burned for their ceremonial scent, all the while chanting words of remembrance and acceptance.

On the third day, Two-feathers constructed a mortar out of clay and dead grass. He slowly kneaded the mixture next to the fire inside the teepee, while spring rain fell outside. It was his intention to seal the opening of the sacred tree and preserve his mother's final resting place. When the mortar was ready he decided to take one final gaze at his mother's bones. The rain fell against his back as he squeezed the front of his torso into the tree. After a few minutes his eyes adjusted to the darkness. He whispered his final goodbye. But just as he was about to leave, the sun appeared from behind a cloud, even as the rain continued to fall. A ray of the sun's light pierced the darkness within the tree and reflected off something shiny among the bones of his mother's ribs. Curious, Two-feathers reached inside and picked up the shiny piece. It was a smooth, turquoise stone pendant attached to a strip of leather. Powerful memories flooded his head. The little stone, with a woman's face etched into it, was familiar to him. Images of it dangling above his outstretched arms came to him. Had not his mother bent over his bed with the shiny stone swinging above him? Hadn't he reached for it while she spoke loving words to him, and sang to him?

Two-feathers felt the wound tear fresh in his heart as he squeezed the stone in his palm. But the pain faded quickly, like waking from a hurtful dream, and he thanked his mother's spirit for the precious gift, fitted the stone around his neck and began to seal the tree.

—

The evidence of trading parties showed as Two-feathers grew closer to the bluecoats' great village. Old campsites littered the woods. Drinking jugs, discarded snowshoes, broken sleds and tools stuck out of the snow here and there. The woods became thin. For every tree now there were two or three stumps. Had the bluecoats come so far to feed the fires of their village? As cautious as a fox he examined everything he passed. He would not walk blindly into a place he did not know, amongst a people with whom he did not belong. But soon he came upon a small group that included some of his own people. There were two older warriors, a younger one and a couple of white-skinned warriors. All were acting strangely. At first he thought they were sick. They were swaying back and forth and falling down. But they were also singing and laughing and shouting. After he watched them for a while he realized they were also drinking, just like the redcoats he had passed, only this drink was making them lose their minds. Two-feathers remembered the warnings of his elders and felt that he should help these warriors, even though they were older than him. And so he strode right into their company, pulled the drink from their hands and started spilling it onto the ground.

"No! No!" shouted the warriors. "What are you doing? Stop!" They swung at him in an effort to stop him. But he easily avoided their blows.

"This drink is making you sick," said Two-feathers.

"No!" they screamed. "This is good drink! This is very good drink! Who do you think you are, taking our drink away? Give it back. This is ours. Who are you?"

"I am Mi'kmaq," said Two-feathers. "Like you."

"No!" said an older warrior. "You are not Mi'kmaq. You are Métis. Your father is a Frenchman. I see it in your face. Your blue eyes."

"I am looking for my father," said Two-feathers. "That is why I have come."

The men started to laugh. "You are looking for your father? Amongst the French? You will have to look at many men, my son. Perhaps you will find that you have many fathers."

They laughed harder. Two-feathers felt insulted but did not want to show it. He had never seen Mi'kmaq behave this way. He felt embarrassed for them and wanted to leave.

"Ah, come and have a drink with us, young warrior. Come and taste the French drink. You will like it. Come! Come and drink with us!"

"No!" said Two-feathers. "I will not drink that poison. I will leave now. I wish you many safe days of travel and many blessings."

"But we are not going anywhere! Come! Come and drink with us!"

Two-feathers waved respectfully and walked away. He was upset and confused. He had never seen Mi'kmaq warriors act this way before. They had called him "Métis," which meant "mixed blood." It was true; he was of mixed blood. But no Mi'kmaq had ever said that to his face before. No one had ever suggested he didn't belong. It was a disturbing thought. If he didn't belong with the Mi'kmaq, with whom did he belong? It surely wasn't the blue-coats.

He crossed a hill and picked up the taste of salt in the air. Climbing to the top of a tree, he saw the great water spread out at the base of the sky. In the distance were little huts here and there with fires burning. More distantly, jutting into the great water was the bluecoats' village. From a distance it didn't seem so impressive, but what *was* impressive was how much of the woods had been consumed. Fields of stumps spread out as far as he could see and beyond. New, fledgling trees had sprouted. From field to field he could judge the age of the cutting by the height of the new trees. The bluecoats had been cutting trees for twice his age.

To the right, closest to the great water, was a swamp where no trees grew at all. This would be the least desirable approach to the village. No one would ever camp there. This was the way he would go.

Chapter Seven

She sat stiffly, held the bow too tightly and cradled the violoncello so awkwardly between her knees she looked like she was trying to climb a tree. Yet she put her heart and soul into playing a little song by an old French master that might have sounded pleasant if the bow had been tightened enough, rosined enough and she didn't pull it crookedly across the strings so that the tone was dry and shallow, like the breathing of a dying invalid. She was trying so hard. How on earth she had managed to stay sane at Louisbourg was beyond me. She had courage.

"It makes me feel happy when I play," she said nervously, "but I'm not very good at it."

I smiled politely. "You're not so bad. Would you mind if I tried it?"

"Please! I would love to hear what it is supposed to sound like."

I picked up the violoncello. It was light, delicate and designed like a perfect pear. I saw from the inscription inside the belly that it had been made by one of the best craftsmen in Paris. I tuned it, tightened the bow, rosined it, took a seat opposite her and held the instrument between my knees. The memory of my father throwing my own violoncello into the sea flooded me as I shut my eyes and pulled the bow across the strings. It sang! Sound emerged from its belly and echoed around the room like a booming drum. It was beautiful. I took a breath and began the first of the Bach suites.

The bow danced across the strings and the violoncello sang like a tenor angel. For a few moments I completely forgot where I was. Never before had I played with such bittersweet joy, which was ironic considering where we were. When I finished playing and opened my eyes I saw tears running down Celestine's cheeks, though she was smiling and her face was lit like a candle.

"That was the most beautiful thing I have ever heard," she said.

I shrugged my shoulders. "Thank you."

"I cannot believe we were playing the same instrument. It is so beautiful. Please teach me to play, Master Jacques? If you will, I promise you I will practice so very hard. I cannot promise I will have talent, but I will apply myself most earnestly."

That much I could believe. "Mademoiselle, it would be an honour to share my musical training with you."

We started right away. For the first lesson we covered the basics of correct posture and handling of the bow and instrument. We quickly discovered that it was impossible for Celestine to hold the violoncello properly because of her dress. The dress fell in thick folds of rich silk and was bordered at the hem with heavy lace. It showed just how determined she was to learn that she simply raised the dress above her knees, revealing skinny calves, folded the silk tightly beneath her thighs and pulled the instrument to a proper position. This was hardly a fitting thing for a young lady to do and it didn't surprise me that the maid quickly left the room, no doubt to run down and tell M. Anglaise. But she came straight back with a heavy frown on her face and never said a word, so he must have approved.

We continued the lesson for nearly two hours. Celestine had a lot of energy for a sickly looking girl. I think I was more tired than she was by the end of it. I bowed, she curtsied and I promised to return the next day. Stepping out into the promising sunshine I took a deep breath and smiled. Perhaps Louisbourg wasn't going to be the horrible ordeal I had expected it to be. Then I ran directly into my father.

"Jacques! I have been looking everywhere for you. Been up to see the Governor, have you? Well, I hope he has set you straight on a few things. Come now. Hurry! I have found a uniform for you. There are so many things to do. Today is the day, Jacques, the day to set aside all of your childish ideas."

"A uniform …?"

"Of course a uniform! We are a country at war. You will take your part in defending the King from the enemy."

"The English?"

"Of course the English!"

"Some of my friends are English."

"Then your friends are enemies! Wake up, Jacques! Stop running around with your head in the clouds! You will put on a uniform today and you will obey me or I will have you spend a few days in the dungeon. That will straighten you out quickly enough. Don't test my patience, son. Do as I say. It is for your own good."

Anger raced through me as I followed my father to the barracks. I felt my face flush. He lifted a uniform off my bed and threw it at me. "Put it on!"

I was so upset I could hardly breathe. The uniform was made of the heaviest wool and was musty and terribly itchy. The boots were uncomfortable and needed to be worn in. He gave me a tri-cornered hat, which was heavy on my head and made me feel ridiculous. Finally, he handed me a musket and said, "Follow me!"

He led me on a long walk around the fortress. My feet were blistered in less than an hour and we walked for two. He showed me everything, explaining in detail how the fortifications worked, how ingenious the design of the bastions was, how and why the cannon were positioned just so. I wasn't paying much attention because I was so uncomfortable. Then he led me through the Governor's courtyard and up on top of the fortress walls. From there a large swamp spread out as far as the eye could see. In all this time I hadn't uttered a word. But here, from this high point, where one could easily view the entire fortress and all its defences, there was one thing I was curious to know. I couldn't help it. I knew he would be pleased if I asked him a question about the fortress, although that wasn't why I asked; I really wanted to know.

"Why are there no cannon pointed towards the swamp?"

He laughed. "Because it's a swamp."

"But ... what if the English come across the swamp?"

He laughed again. "They can't."

"But ... why not?"

"Because it's a *swamp*. It's impossible to march through a swamp. And even if they could somehow, which they couldn't, they certainly couldn't drag their cannon through it. It is physically impossible. It is scientifically impossible. Besides, the English are a seafaring people. They like to fight on the sea. No, they will come from the sea, my son, and they will face the greatest barrage of cannon fire that ever welcomed a flotilla of war ships. And we will stand by, Jacques, and watch their ships sink in our harbour like paper boats on fire."

I went to bed that night with blisters bleeding on both feet. My ears were ringing from having shot the musket a dozen times or so, and I believed my hearing would never be the same again. My shoulder was bruised from the kick of the musket and my head ached from having spent so much time in my father's company. Here, in Louisbourg, he was in his element. He was happy. But how could anyone be happy here? And how could anyone love war? It made no sense.

It was torture to pull the boots on in the morning. My father was already gone but had left strict orders for me to march around the fortress all morning. I had promised to give Celestine another lesson. After catching up on my letters to my mother, I decided I'd better check in at the Governor's residence first to explain. At the entrance I was greeted by the frowning maid who told me that M. Anglaise wanted to see me.

"Ah, my young scholar. How different you look in uniform. What misfortune man brings upon himself with war. My dear Jacques, I must already thank you. My daughter is in her happiest mood for many months. It is the first time I have seen her smile in ages. I am grateful. She says you play the violoncello in such a way as to inspire her to want to be happy again. That is quite a compliment. She has even taken up her needlepoint again, and painting, and was practicing the violoncello late into the night. How can I express my gratitude to you? Is there anything I can do for you, any way to ease the passing of your time here?"

I looked down at my itchy uniform and aching feet and smiled.

"Well, there *is* one thing ..."

Chapter Eight

The swamp was treeless but covered with patches of thick grass. And there were small grassy mounds and isolated bushes here and there. It looked mostly flat from a distance but concealed many channels that washed away mud and swept it into the sea. Most of the channels were shallow but a few were deep enough to hide a man. Two-feathers dug into the muddy wall of one and created a small cave that he supported with driftwood from the beach and lined with spruce boughs. He collected his materials and made fires at night. He burned the fires beneath a layered spruce-bough canopy that hid the flames and thinned out the smoke. He slept part of the day and part of the night in the cave, keeping warm and dry while wind and rain beat down outside. He prayed to animal spirits to guide him. In the day he became like the muskrat, working with great industry around the water and mud. At night he became like the owl, travelling without weight or sound over the wall and into the shadows of the bluecoats' village.

Two-feathers discovered the village to be just as legend had said: towering, ever-spreading, filled to burst with people, weapons and noise. He saw every manner of person there: man, woman and child; white-skinned and Native; well-postured and slouched. Most were slouched. But he was particularly interested in the bluecoats themselves, the warriors who patrolled the grounds and carried fire weapons. His father would be one of them.

———

He climbed the wall at night and watched from the shadows and learned that the bluecoats kept a constant vigil at two gates. They regularly patrolled the grounds. He watched the soldiers walk in pairs, lost in conversation and paying little attention to what was going on around them. This made it easy to follow them at a close distance in the dark, sit nearby whenever they stopped to rest, and they would never know he was there. They didn't make noise with their weapons at night but made quite a racket with their talking and laughter.

They fired their weapons in the day. Occasionally he was wakened by the booming of the large ones, which did indeed throw stones nearly the weight of a man out to sea. Two-feathers had inspected these mysterious weapons at night, with their long, stone trunks lying immovable like fallen trees, and their round stones filled with weight as if by magic. He lifted a few of the stones and was amazed that they could weigh so much. The firing of these weapons created a sound like the roar of thunder. It made the birds rush into the air.

The weapons they carried in their arms made a sharp, cracking noise that cut the air like trees splitting in half. Two-feathers watched them fire the weapons but they never seemed to fire at anything but air so he could not judge their effectiveness or accuracy. But they certainly made lots of noise. How unlike bows and arrows, or knives, that killed silently. Perhaps the noise was meant to scare their enemies as much as kill them. He watched them practise a few times in the twilight, while he remained hidden in the shadows. The leaders barked orders at the bluecoats with a sound that did not strike him as respectful. As he watched the stiff soldiers stand still and create noise and smoke with their weapons he drifted back in his mind to standing in the woods as a boy, shivering in the cold while an older warrior taught him to shoot his bow; with a gentle but firm voice, he told Two-feathers how to calm his mind so as not to feel the cold. And he remembered the trust he felt then and the deep respect he gained for his teacher, because what he taught him was true. After that lesson, everything else he learned about being a warrior he learned calmly through his mind first. Here now, there was something mindless in this shooting at the air. He could not recognize trust between the bluecoats and their leaders. Nor could he recognize respect.

Two-feathers knew it was going to be difficult to identify his father without knowing what he looked like. So many bluecoats looked the same – pale faces, bristled cheeks, sunken eyes and bored expressions. He did not want to believe that his father looked like this. He knew that there were bluecoats who stayed indoors most of the time. They were more brightly dressed, stood up straighter and wore expressions of greater purpose. His father might be one of them. But how could he get close enough to see? He would have to find a way to enter their buildings at night without getting caught.

Climbing the fortress walls was not difficult once he got used to the grip of the stone. It was a soft stone that broke easily when struck with a harder one. In this way he was able to cut wedges for his hands for climbing. In just a few days he cut climbing routes up several sections of the wall and practised running up and down like a squirrel. From the top he learned the timing of the nightly patrols and was able to enter the village whenever he pleased with little risk of getting caught.

He didn't *have* to enter the fortress secretly; he was not an enemy. He could have approached the main gate just like anyone else and asked for permission. But he preferred not to. He preferred to remain invisible and keep his business to himself.

Climbing the walls of the buildings inside was a little harder because they were constructed of wood and he had to shimmy up them as up a tree without branches. Getting inside was even harder. They had glass windows, which were kept shut, and he could not pry them open without breaking them, which would surely wake the people sleeping inside. Neither could he see clearly enough through the windows to identify a sleeping face. Still, as late spring rolled into early summer he became expert at entering the fortress at night, climbing the walls of buildings and peering in through their windows like a ghost. In fact, many inhabitants that summer had frightening dreams of a ghost watching them while they slept.

The bluecoats were creatures of habit and liked to follow a routine. But they were unpredictable too. They could change their routine quickly and without warning. Two-feathers learned this the hard way.

He had entered the fortress after dark and passed through the town and down to the waterfront to gaze upon the giant boats in the harbour. As he stared in awe at their astonishing size he began to form a plan for swimming out and climbing onto them. There were warriors on them. Perhaps his father was one of them. Returning through the village at the end of night he was surprised by a gathering of soldiers in the courtyard of their leader just before the rising of the sun. While he could have shown himself and simply asked to be let out of the fortress (after all there were other Mi'kmaq there), he decided to remain unseen. At the last minute he ducked into a small shed at one end of the courtyard. There he crouched down, calming two startled sheep with soft words. Unfortunately, the soldiers stayed in the courtyard long after the sun came up, and the sun shone bright and clear on a rare, cloudless day. Two-feathers made himself as comfortable as possible in the straw at the back of the shed and waited.

By mid morning, after much firing of their weapons, the soldiers left the walled courtyard and a peaceful stillness descended upon it. An elderly lady came out and freed the sheep but did not see Two-feathers hidden in the straw. As the sun beat down on the shed and warmed it up, he grew sleepy. Birds sang out and bees buzzed around the flowers in the small garden next to the shed as he drifted off to sleep.

It was the middle of the afternoon when he woke to the sound of light footsteps outside. Someone had come to water the flowers and was singing a beautiful song. Her soft, youthful voice seemed to float upon the air and it reminded him of his mother. Two-feathers sat up, filled with curiosity. Leaning over to peek through the cracks he caught sight of her and was astonished. He had never seen such a person. She was dressed in cloth as smooth and shiny as water but coloured like the rainbow. Her hair was golden, like summer wheat, her skin white like sun-bleached driftwood. She carried a look of such thoughtfulness he wondered if maybe she was a spirit of some kind. She was taking such pleasure in the flowers, birds and bees around her. Two-feathers was mesmerized.

He stared until he was stiff in the neck. Eventually, she left. When darkness fell he was freed. He had spent the entire day hidden in the straw of the stable. He was hungry now and couldn't wait to return to the swamp and roast some meat. But as he climbed down the outer wall and returned to his muskrat den he carried the young woman in his mind. He couldn't stop thinking about her.

Chapter Nine

The problem of how to avoid soldiering and spend my days in the Governor's residence instead was heavy on my mind the moment I woke. It was the key to my survival at Louisbourg. I quickly wrote to my mother, dressed in my uniform, pulled those punishing boots onto my feet and limped out the door. A soldier's day started early, and I risked getting thrown into the dungeon if I were late.

My father expected a lot of me, considering I had never had military training before. The regular soldiers snickered at me, they who had no idea what a pathetic-looking bunch *they* were. They all sat with poor posture and couldn't stand to attention properly no matter how hard they tried. Neither did they march particularly well because most of them were usually sick from drinking the night before. Such were the men who laughed at me because I couldn't get comfortable in the uniform and carried my musket like a shovel. But some of them were kind and offered me encouraging words and told me how to treat my blisters, how to stand for a long time without getting so tired and, most importantly, how to hide food in my clothing for the long stretches between meals.

From early morning to mid afternoon we marched in and out of the fortress, inspected cannon, shot our muskets and carried supplies in and out of the warehouses. When I peeled the boots from my feet during a break I found my socks were soiled with blood. My ears were ringing with musket shot and vulgar jokes. If I hadn't had an appointment to teach Celestine I might really have shot myself and put an early end to a most unpromising military career.

I limped into the Governor's residence in uniform. A servant informed me that M. Anglaise was expecting me. He was wearing a severe expression on his face. "Jacques. I have spoken with the Governor and he has given some thought to your request. I am sorry that I must ask you to reconsider it. The Governor feels that, at fifteen years of age, it is impossible for you, even as learned as you are, to appreciate the effect it would have upon your father were the Governor to command him to release you from your military duties. He feels further that, being your father's only legitimate son, you have a moral duty to recognize his rights as father. While the Governor does sympathize with you and does believe that the man who carries Voltaire and Montaigne in his head will always be more of a man than the one who carries a musket and sword, all the same, it would be a blow to your father from which he fears he would not recover. Such is the fragile nature of men of military disposition. However, he has spoken with your father and explained to him that I do require your services here as well, both as musical instructor to my daughter and to assist me occasionally with my correspondence. This would necessitate that you serve limited military duties primarily at night in the role of sentinel, a position much less egregious, I'm sure. Does this arrangement agree with you?"

"Yes, sir. Very much so. I am deeply grateful for your intervention."

"You are welcome. I do wish I could do more. Alas, by the discretion of our King, we are a nation at war."

I bowed to M. Anglaise and went upstairs. Celestine was sitting in the centre of the room with the violoncello on her lap, cradling it as if it were a pet. She was smiling and looking happier than the day before. Now I could see that she was actually very pretty. She was wearing a different dress, shoes, ribbons and jewellery. She certainly had a flare for fashion. What a waste it was when there was no one to see it but her father, the maids and me.

"My father says I have improved already," she said happily. "Is that possible?"

I nodded my head. "The moment you hold the bow and instrument properly your tone improves."

"I love it. I have been practicing. May I show you?"

"Please."

She gripped the bow with a delicate hand and drew it earnestly across the strings. The violoncello failed to sing as well as it was able, but the tone was warmer than before.

"You *are* improving."

She grinned shyly. "Thank you, Jacques. I am so excited about it. I am so glad you have come to Louisbourg. I'm sure you didn't want to."

I smiled awkwardly. Proper etiquette required me to say that I was happy to be here anyway, but I couldn't seem to form the words in my mouth.

"Am I holding the instrument properly?"

"Yes."

"Is my bow crooked?"

"No."

"Am I playing too loudly?"

"No. Not at all."

My mind drifted to images of my own violoncello. I wondered if it had sunk right to the bottom or floated just beneath the surface. It was made of wood, so like a ship it should have floated. Yet I had seen it disappear under the water. Was it lying on the floor of the ocean now and were little fish swimming in and out of it, making nests in it; or had it drifted onto a beach on a tropical island far away, now lying half buried in the sand, dried and cracking under the hot sun? The violence of my father's action was burned into my memory forever. It had been such a desperate attempt on his part to change me. He really believed he could turn me into a soldier. He was so wrong. Celestine stopped playing and stared at me with a puzzled look.

"Jacques. You seem so far away. Are you thinking about something?"

"Oh. No, I am listening. I am listening with both ears."

"You looked so distracted. What were you thinking, if you don't mind me asking?"

I did mind her asking. On the other hand, she was sweet and friendly, and the more relaxed she became with me the more I enjoyed her company.

"Umm ... my own violoncello I guess. I lost it. But your tone is really improving. You should try a legato étude now."

"Will you play for me? I love it when you play."

"I'd love to."

"I think I learn the most by watching you play."

"I will play you a new piece by George Handel. You will like it."

"But … isn't that English music?"

"Well, Handel is from Germany. But I suppose he *is* living in England at the moment."

"I hate that we are at war. I don't know why men make wars. Please play, Jacques, so we can forget about everything else."

———

When I went to bed that night my head was filled with conflicting thoughts. I couldn't stop thinking about my own violoncello and wondering where it was, which was silly. It had been destroyed and I would never see it again. That was all. Celestine's was wonderful to play. It had the richest tone, a lighter, more bell-like quality of sound than mine had. It bothered me that the more I played hers the less I could remember my own, and I felt like a traitor in a way, which was also silly. It was just an instrument, not a person.

Then I thought of my father, though I tried not to. Something M. Anglaise had said was nagging me. He had called me the only "legitimate" son of my father, and it seemed to me that he had emphasized the word legitimate. But I wasn't sure. Since I was the *only* son of my father, why would he bother to use the word legitimate anyway? If it had been any other person speaking I might not have noticed, but M. Anglaise was very particular with his choice of words. I wished I could have asked him to explain what he meant, but I couldn't. Returning to pleasanter thoughts of Celestine and her violoncello, I wrapped up in my itchy blanket and drifted off to sleep.

Chapter Ten

Like an owl Two-feathers sat on top of the leader's house and stared at the night. From this spot he had a good view of the harbour under the light of the moon. He understood now that the bluecoats did not use canoes on the sea. Ingeniously, their sea vessels used giant sheets of cloth that captured the wind. They let the wind do all the work!

He could see the silhouette of the whole of the village and a few figures moving around it. Fewer persons moved around at night, but there were always some. There were soldiers on patrol in pairs, and sentinels here and there. There were late-night revellers, staggering home from houses that appeared to be used for nothing but drinking. Some were fishermen, who lived outside the main gate and who had to make their way down the long path before they were let out. Some were traders, who slept outside the fortress. Some were Mi'kmaq, like the ones Two-feathers had met on his way. There were also some children, usually with their parents but sometimes not.

Occasionally some of the revellers would fall asleep along the path, which was not a good thing to do because the bluecoats would pick them up, drag them over to the fortress walls, throw them into dark holes inside, and not let them out for a day or two. And sometimes, if the revellers were making too much noise or fighting amongst themselves, the bluecoats would lock them up in wooden frames, trapping their necks and arms and forcing them to stand in a most uncomfortable position where everyone would see them and laugh at them. Two-feathers could not understand why the bluecoats encouraged everyone to drink so much in the first place, then punished them when they did.

In the early summer the windows of the houses began to open. Now he could search for his father in earnest, for he felt certain that, should he stand next to him, he would know him.

He made his way from roof to roof. Once inside a house, he pounced like a cat from windowsill to floor and stepped silently through the rooms, even though the sleeping rooms were anything but quiet. Some bluecoats made as much noise in sleep as they did awake, women as much as men. Some breathed with sounds like a crackling fire, or a sack of stones being dragged across a wooden floor or waves rolling up on the beach. Some whistled through their noses with sounds like baby birds in the nest or the piercing blasts made by blowing on a blade of grass between the thumbs. Some talked nonsense in their sleep, shouting out with voices full of pain and anxiety. Others shook their nightmares out with a great shaking of their beds and thumping on the floor. There was at least one snorer, nose-whistler, sleep-talker or bed-shaker in every room of two to ten sleeping bluecoats and some had more. This made Two-feathers' quest easier, although the noises were some-times akin to the sounds he imagined evil spirits would make, and that was disturbing.

But his father was not easy to find. Night after night Two-feathers returned to the swamp disappointed. He was also grow-ing lonely. It had been so long since he had been with his own people, and though he passed amongst people every night, it was as if he wasn't really there because he never spoke with anyone nor was seen by anyone. He was missing the warmth of friendship, al-though there wasn't anyone in the fortress he wished to befriend. Except one.

But he did not have to seek her at night. He merely had to hide in the little shed and wait for her to come out to water the flow-ers. It was not something he chose to do every day, because once he crawled inside and the sun came up, he was stuck there until the sun went down. And while no one ever came inside except to let the sheep in and out, and he could sleep there as comfortably as in his muskrat den, the summer sun could sometimes get hot without wind in the courtyard, and he had nothing to eat or drink all day. Still, it was a temptation he could not always resist. To gaze upon her, just a few feet away from him, was so pleasant. Then one day she came a lot closer than he ever expected.

The sheep had given birth. There were three new lambs in the shed. Since Two-feathers had visited before and offered words of congratulation, the sheep did not mind him. As the sun rose and warmed the walls of the shed he found a comfortable spot at the back and promptly fell asleep. His nightly travels and broken sleep had caught up with him. It was noon when he was wakened suddenly by steps inside the shed. Opening his eyes, he saw her standing above him, like a spirit on the air. She had come to see the lambs. Two-feathers lay still. He shut his eyes and concentrated upon invisibility. But she began to speak soft words to the newborns and his concentration was broken. Such a pleasant voice she had. Such a gentle soul. And there was her smell, a fragrance of flowers, floating on the air like thistledown. Still, she did not see him hidden in the hay and he might have avoided detection had she not stepped on his foot. But he pulled his foot away and the movement startled her. She jumped back and stared at the hay with horror, as if looking for a snake. He raised his head and stared at her calmly, the way he would stare to calm a startled deer, to keep her from being overcome by fear. She was struggling in the shed's darkness to see the whole of him. She didn't scream. Two-feathers rose to his feet and brushed the hay from his bare torso and limbs. They stared at each other for a moment without speaking. She was shorter, with unbelievably light skin and hair that looked so soft and golden compared to the black, oily curls that fell across his shoulders. Her eyes were blue, like his. He saw that she spied the turquoise pendant around his neck and was fascinated by it. She stared without a word. She wore a shy smile, made a slight bouncing movement with her hands on her rainbow garment, dropped her eyes and left the shed.

When darkness finally fell, Two-feathers couldn't get back to his den fast enough. He was dying of hunger and thirst. He would collect mussels from the beach, steam them in the fire and make a feast of them with fresh cranberries. He would collect water and make tea from the leaves of the bloodroot plant. And while he feasted he would offer prayers to the spirits. He wanted to ask their advice. He was smitten with the girl who dressed like the rainbow.

As smoke filtered through the boughs of his fire canopy Two-feathers offered up his prayers and his request. The smoke split into thin streams, each finding its way separately into the air, so that they could not be seen from a distance. The spirits answered Two-feathers in his dreams that night. They warned him to be careful. To desire anything too much was to invite suffering. The girl who dressed like the rainbow was not from his people. Yes, said Two-feathers, but she was from the same people as his father. Therefore they had something in common. All the same, answered the spirits, to want something so much was a sure way to pain. Two-feathers nodded to show his understanding but was glad the spirits had not forbidden him to seek her friendship. Perhaps he would feel pain. Perhaps he would feel happiness. In any case, he would like to have the chance to find out.

Chapter Eleven

The first time I saw him I thought I was dreaming. My watch post was on the King's bastion, the largest corner of the fortress wall, which jutted out like an arrowhead into the swamp. It was also the quietest corner of the wall, and though I was supposed to stand alert and keep my eyes peeled, I immediately sat down and nodded off to sleep. I only wished I could have read, but keeping a light on watch was punishable by a stint in the dungeon. The only thing I needed to stay alert for was when the patrol guards would pass. But I could hear them coming from a ways off and would jump to attention in time. It was awfully boring, but at least it was a peaceful spot and I was left alone and didn't have to march. The nights were even lovely sometimes because it was so quiet. Strangely, I often picked up the scent of roasting fish or meat from the swamp, as if someone was out there feasting. And then, I saw him.

He looked like a ghost at first. Like a shadow he ran along the ground, then disappeared. It was dark, but I had definitely seen something moving. Rising to my feet, I stared without blinking for the longest time, until my eyes watered. The ghost appeared again. He came through the swamp like a rat, sometimes running on the surface and sometimes underground. He would appear and disappear. I didn't see how that was possible. Lucky for me I didn't believe in ghosts. When he reached the wall I assumed he would go around it but he flew up it like it was nothing. I could hardly believe it. For one instant I saw his outline in the moonlight – a young Native, shirtless, with a bow on his back – then he disappeared inside the fortress.

I should have raised a call of alarm. I should have shouted out or shot my musket. That was my purpose for being there after all. On the other hand, he was a Native, and the Natives were our allies, although they were supposed to be let in and out through the gate just like everyone else. But there was something about him I liked – his magical stealth perhaps, or his confidence or maybe just his freedom. I wasn't sure what it was but it inspired me. I had no idea who he was or why he was sneaking into the fortress, and I didn't care. I liked it. And so I kept it a secret.

—

Towards the end of May, a few dozen French soldiers left Louisbourg in a small group of ships to attack a minor English fortress on the mainland. They didn't look much like an attacking force to me; half of the ships were fishing boats. But they left the harbour full of the spirit of war. My father was among them, and he was excited. I could see it in his face.

They returned a few days later with half a dozen English ships in tow. Not only had they taken the English fortress and their ships, but they took a hundred soldiers captive and brought them back to Louisbourg! As the prisoners were rowed to shore, one group at a time, I saw my father standing proudly with his pistol in hand, his other hand resting on the shoulder of an English officer.

The English soldiers didn't look like prisoners of war so much as a company of men who had lost at cards. And they were treated more or less like that. None of them was put in the dungeon. Instead, they were housed in the barracks and in a warehouse that was turned temporarily into a holding cell. Some were kept on the ships. They were given a daily ration of food and enough space to walk about. The highest-ranking officers were even allowed to walk freely about the town! This, I was told, was all consistent with the etiquette of war, glorious thing that it was.

The capture of the English fort lifted the spirits of the people of Louisbourg considerably, as did the capture of several English privateers at sea. For a while it seemed as though our forces could do no wrong. My father was overjoyed. But he had never read Boethius. The fortunes of life, Boethius had written over a thousand years earlier, spun around and around like a wheel. We should never feel too unhappy when things are bad, he said, because the wheel is always turning and they will eventually improve. Similarly, we ought never to get too comfortable when things are good, because the wheel will surely turn down again. I never bothered to mention this philosophy to my father. I didn't think he would have cared for it.

One person's spirits didn't lift much with the victory – the fortress priest. He was one of those people who always looked gloomy, and I avoided him as much as possible. But one day I happened to notice Celestine come out of the courtyard and turn into the chapel quickly, almost as if she were sneaking in, which made me curious, and I couldn't help but follow her. I pushed the door open, peeked inside, then slipped in and stood in the foyer, out of sight. She went up to the altar where the priest was tending the candles. I heard whispers. I should have minded my own business, I knew, but I couldn't seem to pull myself out the door. Celestine asked the priest a question, and her voice sounded so different. She sounded worried or conscience stricken. With me she was always light and happy. I couldn't help listening, even though I shouldn't have. I had to strain to hear and I felt like a criminal.

"Father?"

"Yes, my child."

"Do the Natives have souls?"

The priest sighed like a squeezed bellows.

"Well, now, why would you ever want to know something like that? That is quite a difficult question, my child. I think you could think of the Natives as being like lost souls, that is, until they are brought into the faith. Then they become Christian and their souls are given to them. Then, yes, I suppose they do have souls, perhaps not quite like you and me, but souls all the same."

"And before they come into the Church?"

"Well, no, I don't think so, not really. But that is our purpose here, you know, to spread the Catholic Church and save those who are lost."

"I see."

"But you needn't concern yourself with the spiritual plight of the Natives, my child. Our Saviour has far greater plans for you."

"Yes, Father."

"Let us pray. We will pray for the Natives, that they will find their souls."

Someone else came into the chapel, so I darted into one corner and knelt down until Celestine left, then tried to sneak out, but the priest had eyes in the back of his head. "Master Lafayette, I am rather surprised to see *you* here. You have come for prayers, have you?"

"Uhhh … Hello, Father. I was just seeking a quiet moment for my thoughts."

He nodded his head up and down, but I could tell he didn't believe me at all.

"Tell me, Jacques, do *you* believe the Natives have souls?"

"Yes, Father, I do. Absolutely."

"*Do* you? Well, now, you and your father are a pair."

"My father?"

"Yes, indeed. Perhaps a little warning is in order for you, Jacques. There are many temptations for a young man so far from home, many vices waiting to entrap you, body and soul. Walk the straight path, Jacques! Stay on the straight and narrow. And remember: the father's sins are visited upon the son."

"Excuse me?"

"Oh, I think you know what I'm getting at, Jacques. You're an educated young man."

"But …"

He made an angry face. "Keep to your own kind."

He turned from me and continued fiddling with the candles. I stared, confused. What did he mean exactly? I couldn't have cared less what he thought of me, but I wondered what he was getting at about my father. Was he suggesting that my father had something to do with the Natives? I wanted to laugh. He didn't know my father.

Chapter Twelve

One night the bluecoats' village was ablaze with celebration. It seemed no one wanted to sleep. The soldiers had been drinking, including the ones who used to pick up the others and lock them up. The streets were lit with torches. People were wandering about, laughing, singing and shouting. Their numbers had swollen. The harbour was thick with ships.

Two-feathers felt the energy in the air. He sensed that no one would care if he was in the village too. The drinking houses were full and so were the streets. Climbing onto one of the long houses where no one slept but where he always found barrels of stinky black mud, coils of rope, wooden beams, heavy round stones and many other things, he discovered the reason for the celebration. As he crawled inside a tiny window in the peak of the roof he was surprised to see dozens of men below. These men were not cele-brating. They were sleeping. Shimmying down a corner of the wall he took a closer look. They must have been exhausted; they were sleeping in their clothes. A few steps closer and he understood. They were redcoats! No wonder the bluecoats were celebrating. They had captured their enemy.

Back outside, he jumped down to the street and passed through the shadows. There were other Mi'kmaq here but none was armed like him with knife, bow and arrows. Nor did they ap-pear particularly able. Two-feathers decided the bluecoats' village was a bad influence on his people. It seemed to make them fat and lazy. They were especially affected by the poisonous drink.

Coming down one street were a couple of soldiers with their arms wrapped around a couple of Mi'kmaq women. All had been drinking. Two-feathers did not like the way the soldiers were touching the women. They were not respectful. The women didn't seem to mind, though, which made it worse.

He followed them until they disappeared into one of the houses. He couldn't help but think of his own mother – loving and faithful. She had nothing in common with these women, and yet he could not escape the fact that she had been here too, many years before. And somewhere in this place his father was sleeping. Or perhaps he too was celebrating tonight.

For the first time Two-feathers walked boldly down the cen-tre of the street. He was angry. Something about the sight of him must have appeared threatening because even the drunken revel-lers who saw him were alarmed. One soldier made an attempt to stand in his way and demand that he hand over his weapons. Two-feathers pushed the man aside and continued on. But he returned to the shadows after that.

He climbed the leader's roof and brooded for a long time. He wished the bluecoats had never come here. Yet he realized that his mother had loved his father for a reason. He thought of the girl of the rainbow whom he liked so much. That helped him to un-derstand his mother. She must have been enchanted by a bluecoat warrior just as he was enchanted by this girl. That made sense. The only thing it didn't explain was his father's actions. Why had he abandoned her?

He felt a desire to see the girl of the rainbow before the night was over, but the leader's house was the most difficult of all to enter. There were guards at the doors, the windows were higher and the walls more difficult to climb. He knew this was where she lived because he had seen her come and go. After several failed attempts at scaling the walls he took refuge in the shed. There he made himself comfortable and waited for morning.

She came out in the middle of the day. She moved quietly, humming softly to herself and swinging a water jug in her arms. She was wearing a dress of silver cloth that reflected the sun like the skin of a salmon, flashing bright colours with each movement. She had raised her hair above her neck and twisted it up in spirals. It reminded him of the baskets the women of his tribe wove in the winter. She did not come directly into the shed but watered the flowers outside, then spent time admiring them.

He sat up. If she came inside he would not hide from her. She had seen him before and hadn't been afraid. If she had been, she would have avoided the shed now. Perhaps she had come inside on other mornings when he hadn't been there. He wished he could speak with her. He would ask her about the cloth of her dress. Where in nature did such cloth come from? He would ask her about her own land. Perhaps she knew of his father? But he couldn't ask her these things when he didn't speak her language.

When her jug was empty she wandered to the door of the shed, fiddled with her dress and then entered. He stood up. She was surprised again but not frightened. She smiled, and he sensed that she was happy to find him there. Had she even come hoping to find him there? It seemed so. He pointed to a clump of burdocks on the hem of her dress. She frowned, reached down and pulled it off. He wanted to touch the cloth, so like water was it. She read the curiosity in his eyes and stretched out her arm so that he could feel the fabric, which he did. The material *felt* like water too. It was magic. He smiled. Standing close to her now he realized that she was not a spirit at all, she was just a young woman from another place, yet the most beautiful creature he had ever seen. Her skin was as pale as snow, her hair as yellow as winter wheat; colours he had never seen on a person before and they were strange to him. Most of the bluecoats were dark-haired and their skin was tanned. Her eyes were bluish-green, like his, and in her eyes he saw something he recognized – the delicate, almost invisible yet unmistakable look of loss. She, like him, had lost something very valuable. He wondered if she was also searching.

He saw her gaze at his hair, so dark and thick compared to hers. Gingerly, she reached out and took a lock of it between her fingers and twisted it. She smiled so sweetly he felt he might melt into the ground. Then her eyes fell to the turquoise pendant around his neck. It was unlike the rest of his appearance and he could tell that she was curious to know where it had come from. She pointed to it and questioned him with her eyes. Two-feathers raised the pendant to his lips and kissed it, then put his hand over his heart. Could she guess it had come from his mother? Her joy suddenly faded and she appeared lost in her own thoughts. She stared at the floor, as if in a trance. Then she caught herself, smiled politely but sadly, pressed his hand quickly, curtsied, and left the stable. He followed her with his eyes through the cracks in the walls.

That night, the spirit of the muskrat appeared to Two-feathers in a dream. It had come to scold him. What kind of den was this he had constructed? Why had he made only one entrance? Where on earth was the escape hole? Why had he not created a series of tunnels? Why did he have only one den? What did he intend to do when his enemies came, or did he think he would have no enemies? Two-feathers apologized to the spirit for having been so careless and promised to make proper tunnels and dens right away. He explained that he had been consumed with searching for his father in the fortress but that he would concentrate now on behaving as a muskrat should. The spirit answered that it knew he had been looking not only for his father but for the girl of the rainbow as well. Where did he think he could keep such a girl anyway, in a den without escape routes? When his enemies came, how would he keep her safe? Two-feathers promised to make the tunnels right away.

When he woke, he made a closer examination of the swamp and all its channels. He watched the muskrats travel through their systems of tunnels and began to imagine creating a similar network of tunnels between the channels that would allow him to escape from anywhere in his corner of the swamp. It would be an enormous task but the muskrats were industrious creatures and they inspired him with their energy. For every two or three nights he spent digging tunnels now, he spent only one searching for his father.

But he could no longer spend a whole day in the shed waiting for the girl of the rainbow, and so he decided to sneak into her residence instead. The walls on that side were too difficult to scale but there were other walls with other windows he could reach, and he could run across the roof. He was certain he could get in; it would be just a matter of finding the room where she stayed and waiting for her there. As long as he kept invisible he could come and go and no one would ever know he was there. Or so he believed.

Chapter Thirteen

He seemed to fly into the fortress like a bat. I only caught glimpses of his silhouette under the faint light of the moon, but knowing now what he was, my imagination filled in the rest. When he flew up the wall I realized he was just climbing very quickly a route he had cut into the stone. I could imagine what my father would think of that. He would shoot him if he saw him. I was sure of it.

He never wasted a moment, never hesitated for a second, always knowing exactly where he was going. And he came silently, without any sound at all. It was my responsibility to report him. And I would definitely have been thrown into the dungeon for failing to do so. But I never did. In fact, I rejoiced in his presence. He seemed to ridicule everything the fortress stood for, making a mockery of it, and I found that refreshing and amusing. I imagined he was to Louisbourg what Voltaire was to France, or Socrates was to ancient Athens: a gadfly, a critic. He climbed the walls as if they were nothing. He came in armed with bow and arrows and eluded the guards, who didn't even know he was there. I had no idea why he had come and I didn't care. I just enjoyed seeing him, the few times that I did. I felt like I was a ghost watching a ghost.

—

For the first half of summer we won a string of victories at sea. My father was ecstatic. I was pleased too, but only because it meant that he was always away. That made my life easier. Then we began to make plans to attack the English at Annapolis Royal. I thought that was a terrible idea, especially because my father told me right away that I was coming along.

"And it won't help you to whine at the Governor, or Monsieur Anglaise, Jacques," he said with a scolding tone. "I've already spoken with them and they have agreed that the experience will do you good."

I couldn't believe that M. Anglaise would think that, and I wasted no time seeking a meeting with him. I had no trouble getting one – he was expecting me.

"My dear Jacques! Celestine's cheer has improved so much and her health has as well. She is always singing now. I am deeply indebted to you."

"Thank you, sir. Is there any way I can avoid accompanying the attack on Annapolis Royal, sir? I am not a soldier, as you have pointed out so articulately yourself."

He looked at me in a compassionate but uncomfortable way. "Alas, my dear friend, I have spoken to the Governor on your behalf. But your father had spoken to him first, and your father is a most determined man. Presently, he is riding a wave of success."

"He has never read Boethius, sir. Our fortunes will change."

"Only too true, Jacques. Only too true. Alas, there is only so much I can do for you in my present situation. We are of similar minds, you and I, truly we are. But my friend the Governor feels differently. Though he has, to my mind, received his position out of some unlucky design of fate, not particularly beneficial to his health I must say. It is a role he must nonetheless play to the best of his abilities. You see, Jacques, we are a country at war. As much as we might like to ignore this inconvenient fact, you and I, it will not go away."

M. Anglaise looked over his shoulder to see if anyone was listening, then lowered his voice. "The Governor's military advisors, your father chief among them, believe it is now a case of attacking or being attacked, with the former holding all the advantage and the latter a catastrophe. As to your joining this expedition, your father absolutely insists upon it. He assured the Governor you would be gone and back within a month of departure. Success is guaranteed. Perhaps, if you give him what he wants this time he will be satisfied and leave you alone. Why not go along, Jacques, and make such a show of manliness as to impress your old man and put his heart at rest?"

I dropped my head.

"I am sorry, Jacques. I do hope you will take some comfort in knowing that these are but growing pains. You will surely make a great diplomat some day and dedicate the greater portion of your life to the prosperity of our beloved France, in the company of learned men and elegant ladies. A month in the woods at the end of summer is not the worst way for a young man to spend some time. The local flora is exquisite at this time of year, the air soft and mild. You could think of it as an adventure. Tell me, where would our greatest writers be without adventure?"

"But adventure for the purpose of killing, sir?"

"Ah, I don't think there will be much killing, Jacques. They took the tiny garrison on the mainland with little loss of life, yes?"

"Yes, sir."

M. Anglaise sighed compassionately. "I am not entirely unfamiliar with the weight a son must bear for the conscience of his father, Jacques. But if it is a weight God Almighty has seen fit for us to carry, perhaps it is not for us to question it so anxiously?"

"Yes, sir."

"Good, then. Don't keep my lovely child waiting. I expect she has rosined her bow already."

"Yes, sir. Thank you."

I climbed the stairs with a sense of doom. But perhaps M. Anglaise was right. Perhaps a month in the wilderness of the New World would not be the worst thing in the world, though I truly did not want to go, not least of all because I knew I might actually get killed.

—

I saw so little of my father during the first few months at the fortress I didn't know when he slept. He was taken up with wartime activities and the reconstruction of the fortress in the places where it was crumbling. The fortress itself was perfect, he insisted, it was just the elements that were not so agreeable. Wind, rain and salt were a vicious trio that caused much damage. Yes, I thought, but they didn't fire muskets and cannon or lay siege or steal sailing ships. Towards the end of summer the English turned the tables on us, capturing some of our own privateers that had captured theirs. They remained in the sea not far away, determined to cut off our supply line. Not to worry, said my father, we were about to strike them where it hurt – overland to Annapolis Royal, their stronghold in the south. We would pick up forces along the way, Acadians and Mi'kmaq, and hit the English with the fury of a hurricane.

Chapter Fourteen

Wet mud was difficult to dig and carry, but the summer had dried the ground beneath the swamp grass enough that it could be dug out with strong branches, scooped into baskets and poured into the channels. Spring runoff had sharpened the edges of the narrow trenches and it wasn't hard to find places to conceal a tunnel opening. Each tunnel was not long, about twenty feet at the most, but digging a series of them was an enormous amount of work. Two-feathers worked very hard indeed. He did not need to be rebuked by a spirit twice. By the end of summer he could cross one small corner of the swamp without ever showing his head above ground. The muskrat spirit was satisfied.

The scent of autumn was in the air. There were apples in the woods and rich tubers in the ground. Now was a busy time of gathering and storing food for the winter. Two-feathers spent many hours fashioning baskets out of reeds. With these baskets he collected berries, chestnuts, acorns, flowers, seeds, apples, tubers and anything else that was edible. He placed the baskets inside the burrows of his tunnel system and protected them with birch bark and spruce boughs. He began to collect wood from the beach and stockpile it. He planned to winter in the swamp, where he knew the winter would be particularly cruel. Survival was all about preparation.

But there was one task for which he would have to leave the swamp and travel inland for several days, far from the fires, smells and sounds of the bluecoats' great village. He would walk until he reached the hills where he would find bears. There he would pray to the spirit of the bear to let him kill one and take its coat for a winter blanket. He did not like to kill such a noble beast but he could not survive the winter in the swamp without a thick fur covering. He would kill an old bear, one who would not be too sad to leave this world for the next.

Before leaving, Two-feathers wanted to visit the girl of the rainbow and try to explain to her that he would be gone for a while but would come back. He wanted to give her something so that she would remember him and know he would return.

He decided the easiest way inside the leader's house was through the front door, where the guards stood with fire-weapons at the ready. All the windows he could reach were shut. He watched the guards for a long time before choosing this way. They stood at the door continuously but were replaced during the night by fresh soldiers. There was a brief moment, when the old guards left to meet the new, when there was just enough time to slip inside, if he were close enough and waiting. That was the hard part, getting close enough without being seen by the light coming through the windows. Two-feathers used an old trick. He gathered a large clump of grass, lay down on the ground behind it like a snake behind a stone and pushed it forward in front of him. Very slowly he inched his way closer. To the guards it appeared as if the grass wasn't moving at all. He crawled as closely as he dared and waited. When he heard the new guards coming, he got ready to spring. As the old guards turned to meet them, joking and laughing, Two-feathers lunged forward and disappeared inside.

The leader's house was different from the other houses. The rooms were much bigger and the ceilings higher. There was more furniture. Everything was clean and shiny, even in the dim light of candles burning here and there. But though there were many rooms of great size, they seemed empty because there were so few people. Two-feathers came upon only a handful of sleeping persons: servants, who slept close to the cooking areas.

Upstairs he found the leader, who slept in an enormous room all by himself. Two-feathers had seen the leader in the daytime, when he was dressed up like a strutting partridge. He was surprised to see him wrapped up in sleep in an ordinary white shirt just like everyone else.

He found another man and a few more servants. Finally, in the last room he found the girl of the rainbow. He knew it was her room because he recognized her smell, like a clearing in the woods where summer flowers were in bloom. But he was not prepared for the sight of her. She was so very beautiful in sleep, so very beautiful, yet there was something about her that moved him even more. He stood and stared for the longest time trying to figure out what it was. Finally, it came to him. His mind went back to the bones of his mother in the tree. She had lain in the very same position in her death sleep. It was identical. Flashes of her brown hair resting upon white bones now startled him. The girl on the bed had white skin almost the colour of bone. And yet, she was breathing. Her body rose and fell beneath the covers. She was very much alive.

Two-feathers did not want to wake her, though he hated to leave without telling her he would be back. That she might think he had abandoned her bothered him immensely. Why did people abandon the ones they loved? He couldn't understand that. He only knew that he could not be that way.

He wished he could have looked her in the eye when he gave her his gift but couldn't bring himself to wake her. She looked so peaceful in sleep, just as his mother had looked in death. Perhaps, he thought, he could just leave it on the bed and she would find it when she woke and she would know he had been there and that he was looking out for her. Then she would know that he would come back.

He lifted the blue stone over his head. She winced in her sleep, made a face as if she were having a bad dream, then settled again. He waited. If her eyes opened she would be frightened, he thought, but only for a moment. He laid the stone on the pillow beside her head. Her hair was spread out like a golden river. Her forehead was furrowed. She was troubled in her sleep. Two-feathers took a few strands of her hair between his fingers. It was so fine. He felt a desire to place a kiss upon her cheek. But he couldn't. She had not given him permission. He took one final gaze at her young face, peaceful one moment, troubled the next, as if she were battling an enemy in sleep. He would come back, he promised her. Then he left.

Getting out of the leader's house was just as difficult as getting in. He stood close to the guards, just inside the door, and waited. When they turned in one direction, wrapped up in animated conversation, he slipped past without a sound and was gone.

He returned to the swamp full of energy and purpose. There were many things to do before he would return. Halfway to his tunnel system, he heard the sharp bark of a leader of the bluecoats. The sun was not up yet but the sky over the sea was turning blue. The barking voice had come from the water. Two-feathers scurried to the edge of the swamp where it bordered on the beach. Standing tall on the grass and raising his head he saw the silhouette of a ship. It was leaving the bluecoats' village and was filled with soldiers. A warring party! The bluecoats were off to fight their enemy the redcoats again. His father *must* be on that ship. No wonder he had been so difficult to find, he was always fighting the enemy, as any noble warrior would be. Two-feathers felt pleased at the thought. He burned the sight of the ship into his memory. He would watch for it to return when he came back. He was confident he would find his father then.

Chapter Fifteen

Annapolis Royal used to belong to us, the French. It had been a French settlement from the start but was given to the English in a treaty from a previous war. Now it was a strong English garrison. Most of the settlers in the area, however, were still French, or rather, Acadian, which really meant French people who had no intention of returning to France. There were also the Natives, who were more or less allied to the French and the Acadians. I was told that this was because the French treated them better than the

English did. If we killed them with disease and stole their land one could only wonder what the English did.

We gathered in the middle of the night, boarded our little ship and sailed out of the harbour before the sun was up. Dreading seasickness like the plague I was astonished to discover I felt none. Half of the regiment was throwing up, but only because they were still drunk when they marched on board. My father, immensely proud of the undertaking, was not very impressed that half of his soldiers were bent over the sides of the ship, emptying their stomachs into the sea. In a show of discipline he barked out orders for the men to stand to attention and forced us to stand for an hour or so until two of the men fainted. It was then I began to realize I was not the only object of my father's disappointment. None of the soldiers in the regiment appeared to live up to his expectations and I quickly fell into sympathy with them.

It was a very curious phenomenon to me the difference between the language the soldiers used when they were sitting around discussing strategy and the language they used when they were actually holding weapons in their hands. In the first case they used words like surround, capture, surrender and imprison. In the second they used words like shoot, kill, maim and slaughter. I became convinced that you really did change a man the moment you put a musket in his hands.

We were just three days on the sea and always within sight of land. The largest portion of our journey would be overland where we expected our numbers to swell with all the Acadians and Natives who wanted to force the English out of their land. All we had to do, my father said, was announce to everyone we met along the way that we were heading to Annapolis Royal to attack and destroy it. Our allies would come out of the woods and leave the fields to join us. Once again I questioned a certain contradiction in our strategy. Why would we travel across the countryside telling everyone of our intention to sneak up on and attack a fortified garrison? I was the last person to possess a military mind, but wasn't anyone worried about losing the element of surprise?

Once we reached our destination, ships from Louisbourg would arrive with additional soldiers and we would storm the garrison. I remembered what M. Anglaise had said about making a display of manliness to impress my father. I tried to imagine it. I imagined myself running into the chaos of the smoke-filled garrison, yelling my head off and waving my musket around. I also imagined getting shot in the head and bleeding to death on the ground. How impressed would my father be with that?

By the time we disembarked from the ship I had befriended a few of the soldiers, to my father's displeasure. Louis, from the south of France, had come to Louisbourg by the strangest set of circumstances. On a voyage to Paris, he had been mistaken for a thief and had been given the choice of spending the rest of his life in prison or joining the King's army. He chose the latter. He was immediately shipped off to Louisbourg to serve his time. Having left home merely to see the city of Paris, he got a lot more than he expected. Louis was big and strong and had come from a farm. He was surprisingly accepting of his fate.

Charles was half the size of Louis. He wore the smallest size of uniform, but it still looked too big. He always moved quickly, and even when his body wasn't moving, his eyes were. They were shiny and bursting with life, though they occasionally clouded over with the thought that he might never see France again. Strangely enough, his story was the same as Louis's. He had been mistaken for a criminal and sent to Louisbourg. Both men strongly professed their innocence and I believed them. It was the same with many of the soldiers, as if they had picked up the same story somehow when they put on their uniforms. But we all had one thing in common: none of us had come by choice.

Then there was Pierre, who actually looked like a thief. He hated wearing the uniform even more than I did. But he said he preferred the New World to France and would never go back. As we walked through the woods he kept looking in every direction as if waiting for a good chance to escape. In fact, I was surprised to learn that, like me, none of the foot soldiers had any particular quarrel with the English, which made us all unlikely candidates for killing them. I think my father could sense this and didn't approve of my camaraderie with them. He couldn't prevent it, though, once we got into the woods and the heavy foliage separated us to some extent. This was the one part of the expedition that I actually enjoyed – talking with Louis, Charles and Pierre as we walked through the woods on our way to kill the English.

"So, tell us there now, young Jacques," said Charles, with a quick turn of his head, "what's the Governor's friend's daughter like, hey?"

The question took me by surprise. But one of the things I liked about their conversation was how direct they were. They weren't afraid to say anything.

"Um ... well, I guess she's like anyone else."

I knew that wasn't true but didn't know what else to say.

"She can't be. Come on, now, a beautiful thing like that. What's it like to talk with her? What do you say to her?"

"The same thing I say to anybody else, I guess, except maybe ..."

"Yah?"

"Except maybe more gently."

"Well, of course."

"And what's it like talking to the Governor then?" said Louis. "Now, he must be an angry sort of man to talk to. Make you shake in your boots?"

"Oh, no, not at all. He's as easygoing as can be. He's pretty sick, though."

"Oh, come on now, it's the Governor. Isn't he yelling at you?"

"No, he's actually pretty friendly."

"Friendly?" said Charles.

"Yes."

"The Governor's friendly?"

"Well, he is with me. Actually, he doesn't talk much."

"Are we talking about the same Governor there, Jacques?"

"There's only one Governor, Charles," said Pierre.

"I know there's only one Governor, stupid," said Charles. "I was only saying that for emphasis."

"What's *emphasis*?"

"It's … never mind. But what do you do, Jacques? You teach her to play the fiddle, do yah?"

"You play the fiddle, Jacques?" said Louis.

"Actually I play the violoncello."

"I play the fiddle," said Pierre, as if he hadn't heard my answer. "Now that's the way for a man to spend his days, playing the fiddle in the company of pretty women. What do you say, Jacques, eh?"

"I guess so."

The three of them laughed.

"I'll tell you what," said Pierre, and his eyes pierced the woods to the right and left of us as if seeking escape. "As soon as we get done with killing all these English down here, we'll sit down and drink a gallon of rum and play the fiddle all night. What do you say to that, Jacques?"

"I guess so."

They laughed again. But I was curious about something.

"Umm … Charles?"

"Yes, my son?"

"If you don't mind my asking, could you … would you … tell me … how many men you have killed?"

"Lord Almighty! You want to know how many men I have *killed*?"

"Yes. I don't mean to be rude."

"Good Lord Almighty! Well, that's not the sort of thing you ask a man, Jacques, how many men he has killed in his life. It's kind of a personal question. But I suppose, since we're here on our way to kill all these English, and, since we're brothers in arms and all, I suppose I could share that intensely private information with you."

I noticed that Louis and Pierre were listening closely too.

"Well, let's see now. I can't count that young fellah who fell off the pier next to me because it wasn't my fault I couldn't swim. And Fredric, now, he died of internal bleeding after a nasty fight.

But that wasn't my fault either, 'cause I didn't start it. Let me see ... if I consider that ... and that ... and him ... and, well ... I suppose all in all total, I guess I've never actually killed anybody per se."

"You haven't killed anybody?"

"Come to think of it, I guess not."

He looked surprised at his own answer.

"And you, Louis," I asked. "How many have you killed?"

Louis looked embarrassed. "Ahhhh ... none."

"You haven't killed anybody either?"

"Nope. Not a single one."

"And you, Pierre?"

He pulled out a cross from around his neck and kissed it. "No, thanks be to the Lord, I haven't killed nobody."

We walked along in silence.

"But we sure are going to kill those English!" burst out Louis after a while.

"Don't you know it," said Charles. "We're going to blast them to Kingdom Come."

Chapter Sixteen

The bears had grown fat over the summer. They feasted on the same diet Two-feathers was eating: berries, fish, roots and seeds. But the bears showed no waning of appetite. The more mature among them knew only too well what a winter would bring, what being without food would do to their bodies and how thin they would be when they emerged from their caves in the spring. And so, they kept continually on the move in the wooded hills, rooting through every corner to taste the fruits of the season of plenty.

The bears did not seem alarmed when Two-feathers appeared among them. So attuned to the woods was he, he did not bring into their world any sounds, sights, smells or movements that might disturb them. He did, in fact, act as bear-like as possible, without challenging their ownership of the area. He kept a respectable distance until they got used to him enough to ignore him. And all the while he prayed to the great bear spirit.

He asked for permission to kill an old bear. He explained why he needed the coat and promised to honour the bear by making a neckpiece out of its claws and wearing it on ceremonial occasions. Two-feathers wanted the largest coat he could find. He also wanted to make bear-fur leggings. With such clothes he would be able to sit comfortably in his den in the wintertime. He would sleep with warmth and not shiver. He also asked for the strength and swiftness to kill the bear but not for the courage. The courage he promised to provide himself. He knew that the great bear spirit would not take him seriously if he came asking for courage. It was a very long prayer that went on for days. Two-feathers wanted to impress the spirit with his sincerity.

But killing a bear was no small feat. Typically, warriors killed a bear together, not alone. Two-feathers crafted ten strong arrows with heavy stone tips. These were short-range arrows designed to sink deeply into the bear. If he managed to get five of them into the bear he would do well. Then he fashioned a long spear, not for throwing but for stabbing. The arrows would wound and enrage the bear but not kill it, at least not right away. Only the spear into the bear's heart would kill it before the bear killed him. An old bear would be slower than a young bear but smarter, and that made it more dangerous.

It took several days to choose the right bear. When he saw it, he knew right away. So did the bear. It returned Two-feathers' look with a stare of profound resignation. It didn't run from him, though it looked like it would have liked to. Instead, it tried to scare him away with a show of strength. It stood tall on its hind legs and scratched at the trees to indicate its impressive height. It growled low and deep and as frighteningly as possible. It grabbed hold of fallen logs with its claws and tossed them around like they were dry leaves. None of this intimidated Two-feathers. He stayed around as if they had made a sacred pact, which they had in a way, because the bear had also communicated in its first frightened glance at him that it was old and tired and ready to leave this world for the pleasures of the next. Nevertheless, its dignity required it to go out with an impressive display of strength.

When Two-feathers finished his preparations and prayers he spoke to the bear from across a clearing. He offered his most sincere apology and thanked the bear for its great generosity. He told it he was proud to fight such a powerful bear. It would be sad before and after the killing, he said, for both of them, but not during the fighting. During the fighting everything was courage.

The first arrow struck the bear at the top of the shoulder and pierced the muscle. The bear flinched, as if stung by a bee, then spun around in great anger. Before it could charge, a second arrow struck close to the same spot, deeply wounding the shoulder. Now the bear felt panic and rage. It began to run towards Two-feathers. Two-feathers stood his ground and let a third arrow fly, but the wily bear ducked beneath it and the arrow only grazed its head. The bear was dangerously close. Two-feathers let fly a fourth arrow and it sank into the bear's neck, without showing any effect. Two-feathers started to run, then turned and let one more arrow fly, piercing the shoulder once again. This time the shoulder collapsed and the bear rolled into a somersault. It rose to its feet, breathing heavily, and moaned. Two-feathers sank another arrow into its neck, this time right under the jaw. The bear twisted its head side to side and tried to pull the arrow free with its claws. Two-feathers ran to the side to get a better shot. A seventh arrow slipped through the fur on top of the bear's head. The bear stared at him, panting heavily, wanting it to be over. It charged again, but it was a desperate charge, without conviction. Two-feathers aimed carefully and let his eighth arrow fly. The arrow went deeply into the other shoulder and the bear went down again. Two-feathers came closer and aimed once more for the neck. The arrow disappeared into the fur and the bear began to choke on its own blood. The end was near.

Out of respect, Two-feathers tried to kill the bear as quickly as he could. But it wasn't easy. He approached with the spear, but the bear kept spinning around, preventing him from getting a shot at its heart. He needed the spear to pierce the heart, otherwise the bear would die very slowly, which was unkind. He tried to stir the bear by sinking one more arrow into its shoulder. But the bear only winced in pain and acceptance of its coming death. Two-feathers couldn't get closer.

Standing, facing the bear, feeling that he owed it a quicker death than this, Two-feathers suddenly ran in and stabbed at it with the spear. But the bear showed the wisdom of its years and turned so that the spear missed it entirely. Suddenly the situation turned very dangerous for Two-feathers. He was too close. He had no arrows left. He could not outrun even a wounded bear. With a powerful burst of energy the bear sprang at him. Two-feathers could only draw his knife and strike for the heart as the bear knocked him to the ground.

His knife struck the heart on the second stabbing, but not before the bear mauled him with its claws and teeth. The teeth were not the problem; the arrows in the bear's throat prevented it from causing Two-feathers much harm that way. But its claws dug deeply into his chest. If he had not struck the heart with the knife the bear would have killed him before it died. But the bear died first. Two-feathers felt its last breath leave and the bear lie still. He crawled out and examined his wounds. The gashes were deep and he was bleeding a lot but he would survive. He would have scars, but would wear them with honour, in memory of the bear.

He offered a prayer of gratitude to the bear and complimented it for its courage and cunning. He wished it a happy life in the next world. Then he went to the river to wash out his wounds and dress them. He gathered mud and plants and made a paste and applied it to his skin. The wounds began to sting. He laughed. The bear had not been willing to leave without giving him a taste of his own medicine. Fair enough, he thought.

It was extremely painful for him to skin the bear but he did not want to wait for fear other animals would come and dishonour the bear by ripping it apart and scattering its bones. Carefully, painstakingly, he cut the pelt off the bear in one piece and removed the claws. Then he made a firepit and lined it with stones. He collected wood, ignited a large fire and dragged the bear's skinned body onto it. All night he burned the bear, adding wood continually and sitting close by and offering prayers of gratitude. By the morning there was nothing left but bones. He gathered them and made a pile in a trough in the river, where no animals would ever disturb them. Then he began the difficult task of scraping the pelt.

He tied the pelt between two trees and stretched it tight. With his knife he began to scrape the flesh from the inside of the pelt until he got down to a smooth under-layer of skin that would dry soft and comfortable against his own skin. The fur on the other side was heavy and thick, the warmest covering known to him. Exhausted from his work and wounds, Two-feathers stayed by the stretched bear pelt for several more days, protecting it and letting it dry. When it was ready he cut it down, rolled it up, strapped it to his back and began the journey back to the swamp.

Chapter Seventeen

We squeezed into the hall, a whole regiment of sweaty soldiers, a couple dozen local settlers, their wives and children. The local priest said a prayer and blessed the King of France. Then he gave the floor to my father and asked everyone to listen to him closely. The crowd was in a good mood. The locals weren't used to visitors, and as unsightly and smelly as we were, we seemed to make an impression upon them.

My father began by declaring that he knew the King personally and that the King had taken a special interest in the settlers of Acadia. This had a strong effect. "*Vive le Roi!*" they shouted. He then told them that we were at war with the English. There were gasps of surprise. This was because the English were planning to attack France and Acadia and destroy them, he said. My father paused to let this terrible thought find a home in their imaginations. French people everywhere were rallying to the defence of France and Acadia, he said.

There was a particularly determined group of English soldiers stationed at Annapolis Royal, said my father, who were preparing at this very moment to attack and annihilate all the local settlers of French origin and steal their land. Curses were heard throughout the room. My father paused. It is our Holy duty, he continued, to march against Annapolis Royal, defeat the wicked English and keep Acadia free and God-fearing. Join us, my father pleaded. Bring your muskets and pitchforks. Bring your fathers and your sons. Come with us to annihilate the English.

The hall shook with a roar of shouting. "Annihilate the English! Annihilate the English! *Vive le Roi! Vive le Roi!*"

While I knew my father did not always tell the truth, I was surprised at the extent to which he lied to the audience gathered there. He said that England had declared war on France, when in fact it was the other way around. He said that he knew the King personally, which was completely untrue. And he said that the soldiers we were on our way to kill were particularly vicious, with no purpose other than to kill the settlers and take their land. Well, judging from the group we had taken prisoner from the little fort on the mainland, who had given up without much fight, I seriously doubted the viciousness of the garrison at Annapolis Royal.

All of the settlers agreed to join us. It was a unanimous display of patriotism. My father was moved to tears. He went around slapping the backs of fathers and sons and eagerly urged them to get a good night's sleep so they would be prepared to leave the next morning. It was a week's journey by foot. They could expect to return in little more than a fortnight. My father did reluctantly agree, however, after much coaxing, that a short bit of music and toasting wouldn't be out of order. He went off to bed. The weight of a commanding officer's conscience, he confessed, required adequate sleep. And so, amid cheers and salutes to the King and the coming assault on Annapolis Royal, my father and two more officers of the *Compagnies franches de la Marine* went to bed.

There was a moment of silence after they left the room. Then, as if out of nowhere there appeared half a dozen fiddles, spoons, drums and jugs of rum. Nothing in my life prepared me for what happened next.

One man started playing the fiddle. I recognized the music right away – an old French folk tune – but the rhythm was freer than I knew it. Another man joined in. Then a lady began to slap a pair of spoons against her knee. It was the funniest thing to look at, but when I shut my eyes, the clicking made a nice rhythm and actually sounded pretty good. The jugs of rum were passed around and one was shoved into my hands. I politely declined, but Louis, Charles and Pierre appeared, took the jug and held it over my head.

"Drink!" they ordered. "Or we'll pour it on your head!"

I took a sniff at the bottle and winced.

"Drink!" yelled Charles.

I raised the bottle and took a drink. The liquid ran into my throat and burned all the way down into my stomach.

"Great stuff, eh?" said Charles, and he took a long drink and passed the jug on. Soon the room started to spin. The music got louder. People started dancing, singing and clapping. Everyone was smiling and laughing. We took off our jackets. The women removed their shawls. Everyone spread out against the sides and corners of the hall to create an open space in the middle where people could dance. And did they dance! They hopped and skipped and spun around and did somersaults on the floor! I was amazed at the wildness of the fiddle playing too. The fiddlers seemed to be making it up as they went along. It was simple but so full of energy I just couldn't keep my feet still. And the rum heated us up until we were all red in the face and hot in the head. After a while I couldn't stand it anymore; I had to either run out of the hall and get some fresh air or jump into the middle of the circle and join the craziness. To my own amazement, I found myself in the circle, jumping, clapping and swinging around foolishly like a clown. I saw the faces of men and women I didn't know, and yet everyone seemed like my friend. We danced and jumped and kicked for hours. People grabbed me by the hands and swung me around and around and let me go, and then I was caught by the next person, who did the same. On and on it went, while I laughed myself silly.

Eventually the morning came – early and cruel. I felt the worst pain in my head and was sick to my stomach. If this was what the soldiers were experiencing on a regular basis I had more appreciation for their suffering. I promised myself I would never do it again. Many people had stayed up all night. Those of us who had slept at all did so right on the floor of the hall. My father came in and he was furious. I saw him open his mouth to yell, then catch himself. We were there, after all, to recruit the locals, not to upset them, and so he bit his tongue. But I could tell that he was boiling up inside.

It took about an hour to get us all together, on our feet and in some semblance of order. I felt absolutely awful from my head to my toes but especially in my head and stomach. I regretted everything about the night before and again vowed I would never do it again. My father made a quick count of us and came up one short.

"No matter," he said, "whoever it is will show up soon enough. Let's collect the new recruits and get on our way."

Well, strangely enough, they could not be found. Everyone had gone home. My father split us up into several groups and sent us out to the farms of the settlers to ask the men to make good on their pledges from the night before. At every house we entered we encountered the same story – the men were very, very sorry but simply could not honour their pledge because of circumstances that had arisen unexpectedly. One settler's horse had suddenly gone lame, another's wife was about to give birth any day, another's potatoes had to come in before the frost. They were all terribly sorry, but would we like to come in for a drink, perhaps?

By the late afternoon, not only had we not received a single new recruit, we were still one man short. That man, it turned out, was Pierre. That didn't surprise me. I vaguely remembered seeing him take a fancy to a particular girl on the dance floor the night before.

As evening settled, my father was in such a fit of rage I thought he would burst or even shoot somebody.

"Should we prepare to bed down in the hall again tonight, sir?" asked one of the soldiers.

"No!" screamed my father. "We leave now! We'll camp in the woods!"

I confess I felt a little bit sorry for him then. It was hard not to. He was filled with so much determination and was trying so hard to do his duty. But his determination went against the grain of almost everyone else on the expedition. His duty included killing people, and that was insane to me. I still could not believe we were travelling to Annapolis Royal to do that.

Watching my father was a little bit like watching a spoiled child who got excited when things went his way but threw a tantrum when they didn't. For the first half of the summer things had gone his way. Now, on this ridiculous expedition to Annapolis Royal, they weren't.

Chapter Eighteen

The warmth of summer faded like a fire going out. It became wet, windy and cold. The troughs that cut through the swamp lost what little dryness they had gained over the summer and became shallow streams of water and mud. But inside Two-feathers' tunnels he was able to stay mostly dry. This was the muskrat world – damp, slippery passages of mud between dens, and a dark, recessed cave in which to dry out.

The wet mud was a challenge for Two-feathers, especially as the weather turned colder. In fact, this combination of wetness, cold and wind was a scourge to all furless creatures. In some ways the winter was easier because, though it was colder, it was drier as a rule, and the ground was frozen. Autumn in the swamp, with its incessant rain, was a miserable time.

But Two-feathers had created a refuge of dryness, and he thanked the muskrat spirit many times for showing him how to live in the swamp properly. The tunnel floors, which would have become impassably slippery with the water he carried in himself, he lined with branches and birch bark. Inside each entrance he kept sticks for scraping off the mud that collected on his arms and legs.

Fire making became much more difficult in the rain and rising troughs. He reserved one den just for this purpose. It was intentionally unconnected to the tunnel system so that, should it ever be discovered, it would not lead his enemies anywhere. At the opening of this den he constructed an elaborate fire and canopy system made out of logs, stones, boughs and bark. The fires were built on an elevated platform, above the running water but below the swamp surface, and the smoke rose and spread out thinly, so as not to be seen from the distance. He only lit fires at night, when the smoke would be invisible.

In the flickering light of a late-night fire, while the rain beat down outside, Two-feathers sat comfortably in his fire-den entrance and began to fashion two necklaces from the bear's claws. The one with the largest claws he made for himself. The smaller one he made for the girl of the rainbow. He didn't intend to visit her until his wounds had healed more. His chest looked like the troughs that cut through the swamp, and he didn't want to frighten her.

Cutting thin strips of leather from the bear's skin he punctured holes in the claws with the point of a sharpened stone, smoothed them by rubbing them with soft stone, then fitted the leather through. In between he added coloured stones that he had been collecting for years. When they were done, the necklaces would sing the bear's praises, telling of its courage and generosity. And they would be beautiful.

He also wanted to wait because he was sore and feared that the strenuous work of climbing in and around the bluecoats' village would open his wounds again. So for several more days he sat and rested comfortably in his den, fashioning the necklaces and sewing his winter coat and leggings while the rain came down and the wind blew in from the sea.

The day he decided to see her he went for a swim in the ocean. The water was very cold but good for his wounds, and he wanted to wash the smell of mud from his body. He washed his hair, cleaned his nails, filed them with a stone, and rubbed the spruce gum from his hands. Smelling like the woods, not the swamp, he hung both necklaces around his neck and went to see her.

Getting inside the leader's house was easier than before. The guards had loosened their attention and become less careful. Two-feathers felt a change in the energy of the village, though he didn't know why. It was mid autumn; the air was colder, the days shorter. But it wasn't that. Many soldiers were away. They had left on the ship that must also have carried his father. But it wasn't that either. As he watched the guard leave his post at the leader's door – it was guarded by only one soldier now – and move quickly to meet his relief and gobble up a piece of bread handed to him, Two-feathers realized what it was. The soldiers were hungry. The village was hungry. The season of plenty had passed and they were not prepared for the winter. He thought of all the redcoats being kept prisoner, who needed to be fed; it wasn't hard to understand why there was a shortage of food. To run out so early in the season meant the winter would be very harsh indeed. Many people would die, especially the young and the old. And while this was nature's way – it held no favourites – he had expected the bluecoats to know better and be better prepared. He already considered the size of their village foolish. The spirits would never bless such a gathering of people in one area for so long. The animals, trees and plants would disappear, as indeed they had. Why didn't the bluecoats know this? They should have known this. He questioned their ability to survive in this land. While they appeared to try hard in some ways, they did not appear to have the wisdom required for survival here.

He went upstairs and passed the snoring leader. The rooms were so big and empty and it amazed him to see them again. He picked up the scent of flowers in the air and knew the girl of the rainbow was there. He entered the room where he had found her before and there she was, curled up in bed. Again she reminded him of his mother. Her hair lay across her shoulders as she slept. He liked her hair down. It looked more natural to him. He spotted the blue stone around her neck. She was wearing it. That pleased him. He was glad he had given it to her. Her face in sleep was a child's face, so different from how it was when she was awake, and he wondered if she had been forced to grow up too quickly, as many children were, as he had been. And yet, though she was about the same age as him, there was something about her that seemed older too, something that showed only when she was awake. She carried a wisdom that was foreign to him. He didn't know what it was but suspected maybe it was natural only to women. He believed his mother would have had it. He admired it.

He didn't want to wake her but didn't want to hurry away either. Gently, he sat on the bed and watched her sleep. Her face twisted into a frown suddenly, then relaxed. Her brow would furrow, then spread evenly again. Her sleep was filled with dreams, difficult ones. And then, she woke. She sat up quickly, saw him and was startled. Her forehead showed her anxiety. But as the dream trailed away, her face softened, she beamed and threw her arms around him and hugged him tightly. He was startled too and didn't know what to do. Her squeeze pressed his wounds and he winced. She pulled back, alarmed, staring questioningly into his eyes. He smiled to reassure her. She saw the bear-claw necklaces around his neck and her eyes opened wider. Touching them, she questioned him again with her eyes. He raised the smaller one over his head and gave it to her. She took it gracefully then raised the blue pendant in her hand to show him she was wearing it. She held it over her heart and smiled. Then she got up from the bed, went to her armoire and pulled a large wool frock from it. She carried it over and handed it to him.

"I made this for you," she said. "It's for the winter."

It was the first time she had spoken to him. Two-feathers smiled and held up the heavy wool top. He stared at it and pinched the sheep's wool between his fingers with fascination. She had dyed the wool a smoky grey, a perfect colour for coming and going at night. Gently, she raised his arms and fitted the garment over him. Her face brightened into a smile of deep satisfaction. It was a good fit. Two-feathers stood up and felt the warmth of the tunic. He was very pleased; it was a wonderful present. He felt honoured that she had taken the time to make such a gift for him. With gestures he asked if she had enough to eat. She tilted her head to one side – sort of. He gestured that he would hunt and bring her food. Would she like that? She smiled. He was pleased. He sensed what she really meant was that she would like to see him again.

Carefully, Two-feathers slipped out of the house before the sun. He returned to the swamp with something heavy on his mind. He wondered if his mother would have approved of this girl. He wished he could have asked her. Surely she would have, such a beautiful girl, so skilled with her hands, so expressive with her voice and her eyes. And yet, she was from a distant land and a distant people, as was his father. How he wished he could have asked her. It was also a matter of respect, a respect he wished to show his mother right now at this important time in his life, when there was no longer just one woman in his heart.

Chapter Nineteen

The English knew we were coming long before we arrived. That was no surprise to me. We couldn't attack anyway. We had picked up only a dozen settlers along our way, to my father's profound disappointment. Our allies, however, the Mi'kmaq, came out in force, more than doubling our strength. I was amazed to see such a display of strong, able warriors. They looked very noble indeed and didn't strike me as savage at all, at least not in the wilds of the New World, where they fitted in just like the deer and fox. A Mi'kmaq warrior on the streets of Paris would look savage, no doubt. On the other hand, a Parisian merchant would look ridiculous over here.

The largest part of our force was yet to come in ships from Louisbourg, with soldiers, cannon and supplies. Without those ships we would have made a pathetic spectacle storming the fortress, which the English had reinforced in anticipation of our surprise attack. So we pitched camp up shore and waited for the ships that were due at any moment.

The wait turned into days, and the days, painfully, into weeks, but no ships ever came. I think our allies, the Mi'kmaq, lost respect for us then. We were too weak to make a proper attack. At one point, in a desperate effort, we gathered together and stood on a hill in full sight of the English, just to let them know we were there or, as my father unrealistically hoped, to intimidate them into surrendering. I think that intimidation lasted for about half an hour, after which, when they realized we were not actually attacking them, they stopped taking us seriously and taunted and insulted us from the walls of their fort. The idea that our enemy would not take us seriously seemed to humiliate my father and drive him to despair. I'm sure he would have preferred to attack anyway. But we would have lost badly. Without reinforcements, supplies and artillery, we were forced to retreat with our tails between our legs. I had never seen a man so dejected as my father then became. I couldn't help but feel sorry him. But every time I did, I remembered him throwing my violoncello into the sea and my sympathy was short-lived. It was a long, wet walk back across the peninsula to our ship, and a very sour sail back to the great fortress of Louisbourg.

I couldn't say I was delighted to return, but I was happy to catch up on my letters to my mother and I was looking forward to seeing Celestine again and playing the violoncello. We had become friends. We were about the same age and were both stuck somewhere we didn't want to be and were just trying to survive it. Music helped us to do that.

The day after we returned I went to the Governor's residence and learned that the Governor had died. That didn't altogether surprise me. He had been sickly for a long time. M. Anglaise had left word with the maid for me to wait for him. I sat in the drawing room and waited for quite a while. M. Anglaise was meeting with Monsieur Duchambon, the acting Governor, and the officers from the expedition to Annapolis Royal. There was a lot of frustration over why no ships had been sent to help us. The officers were upset, my father chief among them. I wished I could have heard the conversation that was taking place.

M. Anglaise was flushed when he returned. He motioned for me to sit down and wait a little longer. He needed a few moments to collect himself. He had the maid bring me a cup of tea and a piece of cake. I was thrilled. I hadn't eaten cake in ages.

M. Anglaise came back into the room, stared at me a bit strangely, took a deep breath and sighed.

"Well, Jacques. You and your father are not cut from the same cloth. I guess you know that well enough."

"Yes, sir."

"Did they think we could leave the fortress unprotected, with privateers offshore?"

I shook my head as a way of agreeing. He stared out the window. "They're out there right now, just waiting for a chance to strike."

"Yes, sir."

"And we're getting hungry. We've got a hundred men locked up, Jacques. We have to let them go or they'll starve, and we'll starve. And where do you suppose they'll go?"

"Where, sir?"

"To join the forces that will invade us. That's the nature of war, Jacques. There is nothing personal about it. They're good men, many of them. I've met them before. This is nothing personal. Here's a good political lesson for you, Jacques. Why do you suppose we are here?"

"Here, sir?"

"Yes, here in Louisbourg, the French. Why do you suppose we maintain a presence here?"

"To defend the King, sir?"

He laughed. "No."

"To ... extend French sovereignty, sir?"

"No, not really."

"Oh. To spread the Catholic faith, sir?"

"No, not at all. We're here, Jacques, for the fish, foe the furs."

"Sir?"

"We're here for the fish and for the furs, but mostly for the fish. It's commerce, Jacques. We're here for the money. Beneath the surface of political intention you will always discover the deeper, colder current of commerce."

I stared at the floor. My understanding of commerce was about as good as my wrestling skills.

"Now, the forces that will come after us, Jacques, who do you suppose they will be?"

"The English, of course, sir."

"Well, it might surprise you to know that the English will form only a small part of the enemy that will attack this fortress."

"But ..."

"It will be the colonists, Jacques. The colonists of New England, Virginia and the Carolinas. The colonists are landholders. They are the ones who have poured their blood, sweat and tears into the soil of the New World, and so they are the ones who are determined to defend it. They will defend it to the death. We are just here to make a profit, Jacques. They are here to live and provide for their children and their grandchildren."

"But ... why would they come all the way up here to attack us, sir?"

"Because they think we are a threat. The English have convinced them of that. Many of those colonists have been here themselves on trading missions. They've seen what we have and how we defend ourselves. Our officers believe we sit inside an impenetrable defence system, but between you and me, Jacques, I worry that we might be a sitting duck."

He looked at me with a mix of worry and profound resignation. His words made me worry too for a moment, but it passed.

"Yes, sir."

"Ah, well, they will not attack tonight, I suppose." He smiled. "I believe there is a young lady upstairs very anxious for her lesson."

"Yes, sir. Thank you."

"Jacques?"

"Sir?"

"Food is growing scarce. Are they feeding you soldiers enough?"

"I'm getting by, sir. Thank you."

He nodded contemplatively. I bowed and hurried upstairs.

Celestine was practising when I came to the door. It surprised me how happy I was to see her. I had missed her. She looked and smelled wonderful after my sojourn in the woods in the company of sweaty soldiers. I wondered if she had missed me. She was playing a minuet from Rameau, the great French composer, and it sounded surprisingly good. She had improved while I was away. I was envious. She stopped playing when the maid announced me.

"Jacques! Please come in. Oh, I am so glad to see you. I am so glad you are still alive."

"So am I. Your playing is improving greatly. It sounds wonderful."

"Oh, you are so kind. You're flattering me."

"I'm not. Really, I'm not."

"I'm dying to hear you play again. Will you play for me?"

I was so glad she asked. "I would love to."

As Celestine stood up and pulled the violoncello to the side I saw a turquoise pendant dangling from her neck that I had never noticed before. It looked familiar. I didn't want to stare but could hardly take my eyes from it.

"Oh. You noticed my new necklace. Isn't it lovely? A friend gave it to me."

She touched the pendant affectionately with her fingers. I stared more closely.

"Do you want to see it?"

She stepped closer and held it out from her neck. I leaned over and examined it. It was identical to the stone on my mother's ring. I was sure it was her lost pendant; I was sure of it.

"What is it, Jacques? You look as if you've seen a ghost."

"Ahhh ... I'm sorry. It's lovely. Where did you get it?"

"A friend gave it to me."

"A friend?"

She smiled awkwardly. "Not someone you would know."

She seemed defensive and was staring at me suspiciously. I was squirming with curiosity, but proper etiquette forbade me to ask anything more. I started to play and tried to lose myself in the music but didn't succeed entirely. I was distracted. Celestine was wearing my mother's pendant. I was certain of it. How on earth had she come by it?

Chapter Twenty

It was an old trick for sneaking up on seals and sea birds – a floating hollow log, which looked like any other floating log, yet concealed the head and shoulders of a hunter. From the knotholes in the log Two-feathers had a clear view as the bluecoats left their ship and rowed to shore in their wide-bottomed canoes. He had a good look at each man as he passed. Most looked happy to be returning but none of them was his father. Nothing about them seemed familiar to him. What could be familiar anyway in a man he had never seen before? He didn't know; he just believed he would recognize him.

Then he did. He saw him! He was one of the leaders, just as Two-feathers had expected. He knew it was his father right away, not so much by the look of him as by his movement, the way he carried himself. Something in the way he lifted things, the way his shoulders flexed, was instinctively familiar. Yet there was some-thing about him that was unsettling. From his secret hiding place Two-feathers stared closely at the man who was his father as he climbed into the boat. He saw on his face the look of a defeated man, not a noble expression at all. It was disturbing to see.

He returned to the swamp and prepared to leave for the woods. The image of his father's face stayed in his mind and both-ered him. Into his pack he placed his fire-making stones, deerskin tunic, incense he had pummelled from flower petals, and his bear-claw necklace. As a cold autumn wind swept across the swamp,

Two-feathers headed into the woods. He was wearing his new wool garment.

He walked for two days until he found a pleasant clearing at the foot of a small hill where three deer were standing. The clearing was well hidden and protected from the wind. Far from their usual path, no parties would pass this way. He reconnoitered a wide circumference and collected birch bark and thin poplar trees and constructed a teepee. Though his favourite thing to do was to track animals and hunt, he also enjoyed constructing a camp as a spiritual retreat and invoking the spirits, because they almost always came when he asked them, in his dreams, and each time they came he felt richer. Praying to the spirits took Two-feathers away from the natural world and made him more deeply a part of it at the same time.

He took his time. The more relaxed he was the better. The spirits were always more inclined to keep company with someone who was in no hurry. When his teepee was completed he collected wood for the fire. He gathered stones and made a fire pit. He collected water and went hunting for rabbits, pigeon and partridge. As night dropped early in the woods, he settled in front of the fire, roasted his game and began to chant prayers of gratitude and joyfulness. He did indeed feel joyful. Within the year he had found his father, been led to his mother's resting place, and discovered a lovely girl. While it had not been easy, he felt that things were falling into place as they should. The time had come to ask the spirits some pointed questions.

As the smoke rose into the night and the incense turned the clearing into a holy place, Two-feathers looked up at the stars and began to chant. Firstly, he chanted thanks for all that had occurred in the past year. He thanked the spirits for answering his prayers so often and so readily. Then he explained that he was in search of answers to a few important questions.

For two nights Two-feathers slept without a single dream. He didn't understand. Had he done something wrong? Had he displeased the spirits? He couldn't imagine how. Then, on the third night he had a dream. He was chasing animals through the woods. There were fox, rabbits, partridge, muskrats and deer. There were owls too. They were fleeing from him frantically. Over a fallen log they went. Two-feathers stopped. "Please! I am not here to hunt you, I just wish to ask you some questions."

The animals stopped. They raised their faces over the log, but Two-feathers couldn't see them. They were spirits. They were invisible. "Which questions?"

Two-feathers was pleased to hear them speak. "Can you tell me if the man I found is really my father?"

"Yes. He is your father."

"Can you tell me … is he a noble warrior?"

"He is a warrior."

"Is he noble?"

"In his own heart he is a noble warrior, as you are in yours. But you are not the same."

"Will we ever be the same?"

"No."

Two-feathers spent some time considering the answer before he continued.

"Great spirits, should I approach my father?"

There was no answer. He asked again. "Should I show myself to him?"

"Do you want to show yourself to him?"

"I don't know."

"Then we cannot answer your question. Only you can answer your question."

After taking a rest and thinking over the spirits' answers, Two-feathers continued. "Is my mother's spirit among you?"

The deer spoke and Two-feathers could almost see her face. "Yes, I am."

"I want to ask if you approve of the girl I have chosen."

"Do you love her?"

"Yes, I love her with all my heart."

"Then I approve."

"But can you tell me if she will be with me?"

"No, I cannot tell you that. You must ask her."

"But we do not speak the same words."

"You do not need words to ask."

"Can you tell me, mother-spirit, if I will be happy?"

"My son. Sometimes you will be happy, and sometimes you will be sad. This is the way for everyone. You cannot change that. But you can learn to accept that, and then your sadness will lose its sting."

Two-feathers dropped his head and nodded.

"I will try to accept this."

When he woke, Two-feathers was pleased. He remained for another day at his retreat. Once the ground had become consecrated and the spirits had responded to his prayers, he felt reluctant to leave. Without a mother or father in his life, without siblings or friends, the spirit world had become his family and his friends. His retreats had become a kind of coming home. No longer was it the most important thing whether his father was a noble warrior or not. No longer was it necessary to learn more about him. His path did not have to be the same. His path would not be the same. This much the spirits had revealed.

But he could not stop thinking of the girl of the rainbow. She was as beautiful in living form as he imagined spirits to be in the next world. Besides, he had always been taught that a young man must be with a young woman so that their people would continue. And while it was true that they were from two different peoples, his mother's spirit had declared that love was enough to justify any bond. There was no doubting the conviction of his love. But he couldn't speak for her.

Returning to the swamp he skinned a rabbit, soaked it in seawater for the salt he was told bluecoats loved, then roasted it over the fire. He roasted wild garlic and apples too. He peeled the flesh from the bone, wrapped the entire meal in sea grass and fitted it into a small basket that he strapped to his back. Pulling on his woolen garment he went to see the girl of the rainbow.

Chapter Twenty-one

I hadn't seen my ghost for some time and wondered if he had vanished with the season. The first snow was falling. Perhaps he had left for warmer places. Then, like the shadow of a shadow, I saw him. Like before, he came flying over the wall with magical speed. I thought how different he looked from the Mi'kmaq warriors I had seen on the way to Annapolis Royal. I couldn't say how exactly, except perhaps that they were standing around in the open forest, whereas he was secretive and always in motion, like an animal or a bird. The other Natives had no reason to hide. Why did he?

I couldn't stand still nor sit. It was too cold. There was not enough food in my belly to keep me warm. We returned from Annapolis Royal to discover insufficient food stores in the fortress. The soldiers were already under food rationing. It was so early in the season; I couldn't imagine how we would make it through the winter. Pacing back and forth, not for duty's sake but to keep warm, I watched him enter the fortress and drop into the courtyard below. But he took a different route than before. Curious, I turned and followed him a little. Something about him intrigued me so much. Why on earth would such a warrior climb over the fortress walls at night, in the winter too?

Inside the main courtyard he approached the Governor's house. I fully expected him to go around it, but that is not what he did. I watched for the longest time as he crouched low, just twenty feet or so from the entrance. He appeared to be wearing a jacket. I couldn't see it clearly. Then, when the guards went to meet their relief, he slipped into the house! I was shocked.

At first I was too caught up in the mystery of it all, too shocked by his invasion of the Governor's house to figure out what it might mean. Was he a thief? Was he robbing the Governor's house bit by bit? Somehow I didn't think so. He didn't look like a thief. All the same, now I felt that I must report him. As much as I admired him, my allegiance was to M. Anglaise and Celestine first, and he was invading their home.

But something was nagging me. I felt like I was missing a piece of the puzzle. And then it hit me like a stone. He wasn't going in to steal anything; he was going in to see Celestine! That was why she had asked the priest if Natives have souls. He was visiting her. They were friends. Or they were more than that. I felt a twist in my stomach. Why would she like *him*? Why would she like him more than *me*?

I didn't yell out to the guards. Perhaps I should have. It was my duty to protect the Governor's house. But something told me he was not a threat. All the same, I had to go in after him. At the very least I needed to know why he was going to see Celestine.

I raced down the rampart and dashed across the courtyard. I was trying to get to the door before the guards returned. To do that, I had to do the unthinkable – leave my musket on the ground. I couldn't run fast enough with a heavy musket. So I left it at the foot of the rampart and tore across the field. Fortunately, the guards were in no hurry to return. I slipped inside the door, went down the hall and stopped to catch my breath.

It was dark inside. The candles gave only a weak light and very little moonlight was coming in. I didn't see or hear him but strangely enough I thought I could smell him. It was the smell of roasted meat that I had smelled before from the swamp, and it was wonderful! My belly rumbled at the smell as I climbed the stairs and turned towards Celestine's room. It was strange to be coming here in the middle of the night. It seemed such a different place, like in a dream. It felt like we were two ghosts haunting a house.

The closer I got to the door of Celestine's room, the stronger the smell of roasted meat. He was bringing her food. That's why he was coming in. My curiosity was overwhelming. I approached her door and put my hand on the latch ... suddenly, an arm came out of nowhere, slipped around me, pulled me up onto my toes, and I felt the blade of a very sharp knife settle against my throat. I was terrified. I didn't dare swallow, though I wanted to, and stood absolutely still. His arm was so strong it felt like it could easily break my neck. I would never have had a chance if I had to fight him. His breath brushed across my ear. Then his other hand reached around me, feeling for a weapon. Not finding one, he let me go. For a few seconds I did nothing. I just floated there, waiting. I was more than a little afraid. I stood absolutely still, then, very slowly turned my head … but there was no one there. He had disappeared, just like the ghost he was.

I knew I had to get out of the house and back to my post or I would be in serious trouble. I hurried down the stairs and over to the door. The guards had returned. I waited until they were facing the other way and bolted. But I didn't get far.

"Halt!" came the command.

I knew their muskets would be targeted on me so I stopped. Not only had I abandoned my post, I had abandoned my musket. That would bring me time in the dungeon for sure and probably a whipping. I shivered as I turned around. There, to my great fortune, was my friend Louis.

"Jacques! Heavens above, what are you doing here? Aren't you supposed to be up on the King's bastion?"

"Um, yes, I am. I'm just about to get there …"

"Where's your musket? Oh my Lord, Jacques, you're not carrying your musket. Are you feeling suicidal?"

"No, I …"

"No! Don't tell me. I don't want to know. And coming out of the Governor's residence in the middle of the night …"

"Well, I can expl—"

"No! I don't want to know that neither. But I'll tell you this. The guard is on his way already, and if you don't want to get your hide whipped to within an inch of your life you'll get yourself up that rampart in a hurry."

"I will! I will! I'm on my way already. Thanks, Louis. You're a lifesaver. I owe you a big favour."

"I'll say you do. It's called a bottle of rum."

"You bet!" I said. "A bottle of rum it is!"

I dashed across the field, picked up my musket and got into position just as the guard was coming up the other side of the rampart.

When I climbed into bed that night I couldn't stop thinking about it. That the Native and Celestine had formed a friendship seemed so unlikely, so unbelievable. How did they meet? Here he was bringing her food. But it had been at least half a year since I first saw him and this was the first time I'd noticed him carrying food. And she must have welcomed him, otherwise she would have done something about it already, I knew that. But why? What on earth could they possibly have in common?

Then I wondered about something else – my mother's pendant. Was it possible that Celestine had received it from him? But where would *he* have gotten it? Had he found it? That seemed unlikely. Had he stolen it? I doubted it. I had no reason to suspect he was a thief. Thieves don't carry food into houses at night.

I went to bed with these thoughts spinning around and around in my head. It was hard to sleep. I had too many questions and not enough answers. They continued into my dreams. There was one long dream in particular, in which I was in the Governor's house, only it was bigger. It seemed to go on forever. I was drifting from room to room and was aware that my father was somewhere in the house too, though I couldn't find him. The Native was there and he was hunting me. Yet I knew somehow that he wouldn't hurt me. Celestine was there but she wouldn't let me into her room. She was keeping a secret.

Chapter Twenty-two

There was a bluecoat in the house. He must have smelled the food. Two-feathers knew he was like a squawking bird carrying a basket of freshly roasted meat on his back. But the smell of the soldier was also distinct and Two-feathers smelled him even before he heard him. He circled around one of the rooms then followed him upstairs. Strangely, the young soldier did not appear to be carrying a fire weapon. Perhaps he carried a short one or a knife. But why was he heading towards the room with the girl of the rainbow? Two-feathers didn't like that at all. He waited until the soldier was just outside her door, then grabbed him and placed a knife against his throat in case he might call out. He had no intention of hurting him. Feeling for a weapon, he was surprised to discover he carried none. What kind of warrior did not carry a weapon? Lifting the blade away from his neck, he waited to see if the soldier would cry out. He didn't. Two-feathers let him go and the soldier hurried away.

Now there was no time to visit with her, only to leave the food. Entering the room, he saw her sleeping peacefully. He sighed deeply. He would have loved to visit with her again but would not wake her. He placed the basket by her bed and left. She would know he was looking out for her. That was enough.

Outside he made his first reconnaissance of the village in weeks. The redcoats were gone. The bluecoats must have finally realized they could not feed them and had traded them for food and weapons. Two-feathers climbed inside the building where they had been and went across the rafters. It seemed so empty now. Then he heard a noise in one corner. Perhaps there were rats. He smelled a people smell, but not the smell of the redcoats, who had smelled strong. This was not the smell of soldiers. As he moved silently to the corner he heard voices whispering below. There, huddled in the dark, he found a handful of children.

They had created a fort in the corner by dragging over old barrels, rope and wood, then lined it with blankets and old coats. At a glance, Two-feathers could tell the children were hungry. They wore the lifeless expressions that revealed lack of nourishment. He noticed something else. They were not French. Nor were they completely Mi'kmaq. They were like him.

He dropped into their midst. They were frightened at first, but their experiences had taught them not to cry out. They looked up fearfully and waited to see what he would do. Two-feathers saw their fear and calmed them by speaking softly. He asked them if they could speak Mi'kmaq. They nodded. He asked them where their parents were. They said they didn't know. How did they survive then? By asking for food at the houses, they answered. Was he going to report them, they wanted to know? No, he said. He would never do that. He smelled of food, they said, did he have any? No, but he could bring them some tomorrow. Please, they said, they were so hungry. Two-feathers promised he would. Were they cold, he asked? It was not so bad in their fort, they said. They kept each other warm. They were just hungry. Tomorrow, he said, he would bring food. They could count on him. He turned to leave. Where had their parents gone, he asked? They didn't know. Would they be coming back? Maybe, they said. Maybe they would.

Two-feathers knew it was going to be a very difficult winter for the bluecoats. There was already not enough food. This would make them vulnerable to their enemy. He remembered the redcoats' scouting party from the previous winter. Maybe they were planning to attack. This was what warriors did.

The village was every bit as cold as the swamp, if not colder. The wind twisted around and around in the spaces between the houses and grew in strength. It rushed down the streets with a force Two-feathers didn't often see in the woods, and there was no place to find shelter from it except inside. With the snow falling now and the wind so strong, he did not have to take so much trouble to be invisible at night. No one was outside, not even the revellers. No one was falling down with drink or sleeping outside. Only the soldiers were moving about, and only from their posts to their sleeping quarters as quickly as possible, where they kept their fires burning. The colder the season became, the freer Two-feathers was to walk about the great village at night.

In the swamp everything was frozen and motionless, except for the tiny winter birds that darted from bluff to bush with a tireless energy. The muskrats, like the bears, beavers, squirrels and raccoons, were hibernating inside their dens. When Two-feathers wrapped the bearskin around his body and pulled the leggings up, he could sit comfortably in his den, out of the wind and snow, even without a fire. And this is how he slept.

But in the winter there was much to do. Food and wood were further away, and now he was hunting for more than himself. Some of the things he had stored might not be appealing to the girl of the rainbow, who was used to eating other things. While he felt sure she would enjoy roasted meat, apples and garlic, he was uncertain she would appreciate chestnuts, dried flowers, tubers and seaweed. And so he hunted further afield, often staying away overnight.

The woods were quieter when filled with snow. The quietness was suitable for contemplation, which he was beginning to understand was a skill in itself. Among the things he contemplated were the differences between himself and the girl of the rainbow. He had never considered the world from a woman's perspective before. It seemed very unlike a man's. Yet, as light and delicate as she was, and as unsuited to this land as she surely was, there was something strong in her nature that he couldn't help but respect just as much as he would respect a warrior, and that was a mystery to him. She hadn't, for instance, been afraid of him at all, not the least bit, and he knew he must have appeared like a wild animal to her. He spent many hours contemplating this and finally concluded that it was because of her willingness to accept whatever might come her way. It was in this way, in her acceptance of things, that she showed strength, courage and wisdom. Acceptance of things as they were, not how one would like them to be, was the language of the spirits, which could be understood by Mi'kmaq and bluecoat alike. Such were the thoughts that accompanied Two-feathers into the winter woods. But there were other thoughts too, very different thoughts.

Chief among them was his belief that the redcoats would attack. He knew this would happen because it was the way of warriors. The bluecoats had attacked at least twice and had taken prisoners. It would be a very great dishonour to the redcoats if they did not attack soon. He had already seen them scouting the year before. Likely they would come in the early spring, when the ground was still frozen but the worst of the cold had passed. Then, as the temperature began to rise, the woods would become a pleasant place to travel. That is when the redcoats would come, he believed. And that is when the bluecoats, after a punishing winter, would be at their weakest.

What would he do about the girl of the rainbow then? How would he protect her? He could not take her now, out into the harsh winter. She would never survive. But how would he protect her when the redcoats attacked her village? He would have to be ever so vigilant and watch for them and warn the village. Then he would rescue her. Perhaps they would design a plan of escape together.

There was always the possibility that the bluecoats would defeat their enemy. But he doubted it. When he thought of how easily he could enter the village, how undisciplined and unmotivated the bluecoats seemed, especially lately, he didn't think much of their chances. If the redcoats came into the harbour with their ships, the bluecoats would surely destroy them with their fire weapons and heavy stones. Any warriors foolish enough to stand open in front of the weapons of their enemy did not deserve to win. Two-feathers did not know the minds of the redcoats. Perhaps they were different from the bluecoats, perhaps the same. Either way, he did not think they would be foolish enough to enter the harbour. They would come by land. They would come over the swamp.

Chapter Twenty-three

How I wished I could have had a closer look at him, but that was impossible. I even considered going into the swamp myself, but he had no idea who I was and I might have gotten myself shot with an arrow. How could he survive out there in the cold? I strained to see as far as I could, even borrowed M. Anglaise's telescope glass and stared for hours, but saw nothing, not even a puff of smoke. And yet, I still caught the scent of roasted meat at night. And now I knew it was not my imagination.

The nights grew colder and colder until it became a serious punishment to stand at my post. It was impossible to keep my feet warm, even though I kept constantly on the move. My fingers felt the bitter bite of frost. Like the other soldiers, I squirreled away what food I could to keep a small flame going in my stomach. But the little ration they gave us was not enough, and all the soldiers were very unhappy. There had even been a mutiny one day, which was unbelievable, yet showed just how desperate things were becoming. The soldiers gathered and beat drums and paraded through the streets until they were promised more food and firewood. My father was horrified and wanted to have the leaders executed, but M. Duchambon wisely conceded to their demands and the mutiny lost its strength like air let out of a bellows. I didn't think anyone had the energy for a real fight.

I was so hungry I even considered asking Celestine to share a little of the food our ghost was bringing her, but could never quite get the words out. How could I ask her about things that I wasn't even supposed to know? Some days it all seemed so desperate, the cold and lack of food, and I really did not see how I could continue. The less I got to eat, the more I felt the cold. The colder I got, the hungrier I became.

Other days, when the winter sun came in through the Governor's residence windows and warmed me up, and Celestine and I would play the violoncello, I would breathe deeply and know that I only had to hold on till spring when the supply ships would come from France, and maybe, just maybe I could go home.

I think it was worse for my father somehow. The failed attack at Annapolis Royal, followed by the mutiny, was such a blow to him. Or perhaps it was lack of sleep and insufficient food. Everyone suffered for lack of food, although the officers suffered less than the common soldiers. But no one took military insubordination and failure to heart as much as my father did. It just seemed to kill his spirit. I wondered if he sensed it was the beginning of the end.

We were approaching a year since we had come to this bleak military backwater. I had travelled with the regiment and borne arms against the enemy, which I saw only briefly and from a distance. I had been surrounded by hysterical voices calling for the annihilation of the English, as if they were some kind of plague. And still, after all of this, I saw no difference between us and them, other than the colour of our coats, our language and a few cultural differences for which there was no explanation. But for my father, the Annapolis Royal expedition was a humiliation too great to bear. He would not be truly himself again until the enemy was at our gate and he could dutifully fight.

In the face of all of this my ghost continued to bring freshly cooked meals to Celestine almost nightly. And she, unlike everyone else in the fortress, kept a healthy complexion, much to the pleasure of her father, who continued to credit it to me. What a strange situation it had become for me, entering Celestine's room with a gnawing hunger in my belly, only to see the happy smile on her face, which I tried my best not to resent. I also did my best to hide my growing weakness, but did not entirely succeed. One day it showed its face against my will.

Celestine had been playing for me. When she finished, I stood up too quickly from my seat. The blood rushed from my head and I fainted. I dropped to the floor with all the grace of a chopped tree. Celestine shrieked and rushed over to me. I revived but felt too weak to get off the floor right away.

"I am so sorry," I said. "I'll be fine in just a moment."

"Oh! Jacques! What's wrong? Haven't you eaten today?"

"Umm ... I guess not. Not yet."

"Oh! You poor thing! Just wait here," she said, and hurried off. She returned with some cooked rabbit in a napkin. "Here. Eat this."

"No. I cannot take your food."

"Take it, please! I have more than enough. Truly."

"Are you certain?"

"Absolutely certain! Believe me, Jacques. I have more than my fair share of food."

"Well ... if you insist."

"I insist."

The meat was delicious. There was baked apple too. My ghost was a good cook. I wondered what he would have thought had he known I was eating the food he had prepared for Celestine.

I also wondered how I was going to get the pendant from her and return it to my mother. It was the only request my mother had ever made of me, to find it and return it to her. Here it sat in front of my face daily, and I couldn't say a word about it. In bed at night I invented all sorts of schemes for taking it back, but none of them were any good. The problem was that Celestine was so attached to it. She never took it off. I supposed I could have just come out with the truth. But I didn't think she would believe me. I considered stealing it, because it really wouldn't have been stealing when it belonged to my mother in the first place. But how could I steal something from around her neck? And I would feel like the worst person in the world to steal something from a friend, my only true companion at Louisbourg. On the other hand, how could I return to my mother and explain to her that I had seen the pendant, touched it, but not brought it back? Heavens! Would life always be so complicated?

Chapter Twenty-four

He saw many ships in his dream. They floated on the sea like leaves in an autumn stream. The voices of the spirits rose up in chorus: "An enemy is coming. They will bring bloodshed and destruction. Prepare yourself."

Two-feathers woke from the dream in a sweat, jumped out of bed, ran to the seaward side of the swamp and scanned the horizon. He saw nothing but snow flurries. The dream had been so real he fully expected to see ships. Surely the dream was a warning. The redcoats were coming. He must prepare. But how? What more could he do?

The next day, the same dream. Two-feathers jumped out of bed, ran out into the icy air and down to the beach. The dream had been so vivid. The ships were surely coming. He stood on the beach and stared at the horizon until his body shivered. There were no ships. The next day it was the same, and the next, only each time he saw the ships more clearly in the dream, as if they were drawing nearer. His dreams had never failed him before. The voices of the spirits, a sound like the wind twisting through the trees, had always been faithful and true. And yet there were no ships.

The voices said he must prepare, and so he did. He inspected all of his tunnels and dens, taking special care to make their entrances imperceptible to the eye. To the passing traveller they might look like small depressions, unappealing and not leading anywhere, obstructed with roots and debris. He created several lookout stations within the tunnel system from where he could see across the top of the ground. Then he practised crossing the swamp from every angle, in the day and night. Finally, he inspected all of his food caches, making certain they were spread out evenly in case he became caught in one location when the swamp was overrun with warriors.

But the preparation he was most concerned with was not in the swamp at all; it was with the girl of the rainbow. He knew that the redcoats would bring bloodshed and destruction and it would become too dangerous for her in the bluecoats' great village. But how could he protect her? Would she even want to leave with him? And where would he take her? To the swamp? No, she wouldn't want to come there. It would become too dangerous anyway.

The dreams continued. Always it was the same dream with the same message. But he stopped running down to the beach to look for ships because they never came. Be prepared, the voices said. Bloodshed and destruction were coming. Prepare! How, he complained to the spirits. What else did they expect him to do? Prepare how?

For the very first time, Two-feathers felt angry with the spirits. He felt as if they were mocking him. Where were the ships anyway, that they had been showing him in his dreams? In a dark mood he sat at the fire and stared into the flames. The longer he sat and brooded, the darker his mood became. For the first time in his life, Two-feathers felt the painful sting of doubt. First, he doubted the girl of the rainbow's interest in him. Why did he even think she might love him? Then, he doubted his father. He didn't carry himself like a warrior at all. Then, he doubted himself. Why had he even bothered to come all this way? What had he learned? Finally, he turned inward and began to doubt the very spirits who had been guiding his steps for as long as he could remember. It was a dark and lonely night as he sat at the fire and let these doubts run through him. They entered through his head, spread throughout his limbs and back, collected in his stomach and finally entered his heart. When the doubt settled in his heart, his heart began to ache and he cried out. He cried to the spirit of his mother. But she did not answer. He cried to the spirit of the deer. No answer. He cried to the spirit of the bear. No answer. He did not cry to the spirit of the muskrat. He was tired of the swamp now. He wanted to leave it. He wanted to return to the woods, where the rivers ran crystal clear and thick with salmon. He wanted to climb into the hills where the high trees grew and build teepees and hunt swift-footed deer to feed a whole family.

Eventually Two-feathers cried himself out, wrapped up snugly in his bearskin blanket and went to sleep. He slept long and he dreamt. Once more it was the same dream, only the ships came so close to the land the soldiers jumped out and ran up the beach with their fire weapons, shouting. He woke from this dream in a heavy sweat. He stepped outside and was shocked to feel the earliest spring air. Had the winter carried itself away in the night? No, the ground was still frozen. Yet the air had warmed. Spring was indeed coming.

He ran down to the beach. The ships were coming, the spirits had said. Where? he said. There, they had said. Look harder. He looked. There were no ships. Harder, said the spirits. Two-feathers bit his tongue and travelled further down the shore. There were no ships to be seen anywhere. Enough! He had had enough!

"Where?" he yelled at the top of his lungs.

There, was all the spirits had said.

Two-feathers turned one final time and scanned the horizon to his right. On the thin line where the sky rested upon the sea he saw a small brown sail. Then he saw another. Then another. Then many more. There they were. The redcoats had come.

He raced back to his den, apologizing to the spirits all the way. Forgive me, he pleaded. He had lost his reason. He would never doubt the spirits again. No matter, said a voice inside his head, humans are as fleeting as flowers. Spirits are eternal. The eternal does not take offense from the fleeting.

He collected his weapons and a supply of food. He would warn the bluecoats and bring food to the girl of the rainbow and to the children, but not before dark, and not before he had reconnoitered the redcoat force that was landing. It would take them quite a while to land and unload. There was time. Two-feathers wanted to know what the bluecoats were up against before warning them.

Chapter Twenty-five

The winds of spring. What a glorious thing they were. They carried a warmth that melted the ice outside the windows and melted the hearts of every inhabitant of Louisbourg. Well, nearly every inhabitant. I didn't expect the spring made much difference to the priest one way or another. But the winds had brought something else. I supposed it was inevitable.

A solitary fishing sloop sailed frantically into harbour. Her sailors were firing their guns. English ships had been seen, dozens of them, maybe more. The English were coming. They were intending to invade.

I rushed to inform my father. He had taken to his bed of late — so uncharacteristic of him. He had not recovered his fighting spirit since Annapolis Royal. I stood at the door and gave him the news. I had barely gotten the words out of my mouth when he bolted out of bed, dressed into uniform and reached for his sword and pistol.

"Are the regiments gathering?" he asked, as if I were his battle attendant.

"I don't know, sir. I came to inform you right away."

"Of course. Of course."

I followed him out. He started barking orders even before there was anyone near enough to hear him. For a moment I actually wondered if he had lost his mind or perhaps woken from a dream too quickly. He raised his nose to test the wind, then hurried into the thickness of soldiers gathering. I stopped and watched him go. I was not on duty.

All day the officers and soldiers were busy positioning and re-positioning their cannon. There was excitement in the air. Everyone hung around the quay, waiting for the English ships to turn the corner of the harbour so that our cannon could start firing upon them, sending them all to the bottom. We waited and waited but they never came. This tried the patience of the officers. They paced back and forth, sighing heavily and barking orders. Finally, they decided to send out a scouting party on a small fast ship. They would try to count the English fleet, see what they were up to and get back as quickly as possible.

As it turned out, there were about a hundred ships in all, mostly private ones, and a few bigger naval vessels. Only a small part of the fleet appeared to actually be with the English navy. The rest were New England settlers coming together in a militia, just as M. Anglaise had predicted. My father and the other officers laughed when they heard the news. How ridiculous, how outrageous, that a ragged collection of farmers would come to attack the greatest fortress in the New World. And yet, the ships never did come even remotely close to the range of our cannon. Instead, they landed a few miles down the coast, on the other side of the swamp. Still, our soldiers readied their cannon, practised aim, discussed strategy ... and continued to ignore the swamp. But the attacking fleet did not approach our harbour.

After a day, the officers decided it would be a good idea to send a contingent of soldiers across the swamp to see what the English were up to. Of course my father was going. He ordered me to come too.

There were a few dozen of us. We went out in the afternoon and crossed the swamp in close formation. I was fascinated to get into the swamp and look for signs of my ghost. I had visions of stumbling upon him in some makeshift teepee somewhere, but there wasn't a single trace of him nor anybody else – not a single trace.

On the south side of the swamp were a few scattered bushes and trees that eventually gathered into a short-treed woods, no taller than a man. Before we could enter the woods we caught sight of a flash of red amongst the trees.

"Form a line here!" yelled my father.

He pointed to the ridge of a tiny bluff. It was a good spot to take cover and still see the enemy. Within an hour the English had formed a line at the edge of the woods. They really were a motley-looking group. For every English soldier dressed in proper uniform, there were half a dozen settlers who looked as though they had come out to plow the field. Yet, all brandished muskets. And that was not all. With telescoped glasses, our spotters had seen the English unloading cannon onto the beach.

"Hah!" laughed my father. "A lot of good cannon will do them here."

The cannon were impossibly out of reach, and, I had to confess, the swamp looked impassable. Horses and oxen would not have been able to drag them across it, even if they had brought such beasts, which they hadn't. I couldn't imagine the kind of fortitude and determination it would take for men to drag those cannon across the swamp by themselves. That truly did not seem possible. I remembered the Acadian settlers we met on our way to Annapolis Royal, who had pledged themselves so earnestly then failed to show up the next day. In contrast, these New Englanders outnumbered the redcoats six to one. What kind of motivation was this, to come so far from their own land and risk their lives for such an isolated outpost, imposing as it was? I couldn't understand it.

Before long there was an exchange of musket fire. Small clouds of smoke rose from both sides, with neither hitting their target. I was standing at the very back of our group. Muskets, for all their noise and commotion, were actually terribly inaccurate. To really kill anyone, both sides would have to leave the safety of their positions, move into the open field, where they were completely exposed, and shoot. From my perspective this meant kill and get killed. Everybody loses.

It was a credit to my father that he remained true to the bitter end. There wasn't an ounce of cowardice in him. Under fire from the enemy, with high risk of death, he never flinched nor considered any option other than facing them directly. At the time, I failed to understand him. But I had *never* understood him. From the instant the decision was made to leave the safety of the bluff and step into the open field, he carried himself with conviction and courage. He called for me to accompany him, but he never looked back to see if I did. I stayed where I was. There was no way on earth I was going to put my flesh and bones in the way of an enemy aiming muskets at me, trying to kill me. I didn't want to die. I wanted to go home. I had never wanted to come to Louisbourg in the first place. I was too young to die.

But my father went. And the other soldiers went, and they formed a line. They bent down and prepared their muskets. You might have thought they were kneeling to polish their boots or pick stones or something. They loaded their weapons with powder and shot and took aim calmly and with practised obedience. Then, on command, they shot their muskets just as we had shot them so many times inside the fortress walls. Only this time the barrels were aimed at a wall of men. To my sheer amazement, three or four of the men standing in line opposite us fell to the ground. Almost instantly, three or four others came forward and took their places. Our side was reloading when the English fired for the first time. My father was the first one to go down. I thought he had just tripped, but he fell forward onto his face and did not pick himself up. I was so shocked I did not really believe it. I kept expecting him to get to his feet, brush the dirt from his uniform and continue issuing commands. But he never did. There were several more volleys of musket fire back and forth, but the English seemed to be reloading faster than we were and our soldiers started to drop too quickly. Still, I waited for my father to get up. But he didn't. He never moved. Suddenly, everyone ran back, passing by me and continuing towards the fortress. No one bothered with those who had been shot. If the wounded could make it to the bluff on their own they would have a chance, maybe, otherwise they were left to die. This was the practice of war.

Twilight was falling. My father had not moved. I never heard him cry out. I thought I heard a few soldiers moaning on the field, but it might have been the wind. It was a horrible sound. No one ventured onto the field to help them. Since it had been a while since the shooting had stopped, I left the safety of the bluff, left my musket behind and snuck onto the field. I crouched low and scurried over to where my father was. I hoped no one would see me. When I reached him I rolled him over. He moved his eyes. He was still alive! He had been shot in the chest. Blood poured from his mouth and he had been choking on it. He didn't speak. His eyes were wide open and they looked far away. His pupils were dilated. I couldn't tell if he was conscious or not. Did he know I was there? I stared into his eyes and the truth stared back at me: he was a stranger to me. I was a stranger to him. I had the most peculiar feeling then, staring at him, as if there had been a terrible mistake in the order of things – that he was never supposed to have been my father at all or me his son, that there had been a mix-up somewhere along the way. And then, he faded away. For a second I thought he looked into my eyes. His eyes twitched. He stopped breathing shortly afterward, but his eyes did not close. I knew that was it. He was gone.

I heard muskets firing. I thought they were too far away to get a decent shot at me. Then, I heard something else – fifes and drums – the music of English soldiery. In the midst of this nightmare the music sounded both beautiful and frightening. There was something strangely terrifying about music played on a battlefield. Suddenly a musket shot struck my boot, tore through the leather and pierced my skin. I felt a burning in my foot. I squeezed my father's lifeless hand and scurried like a rat back to the bluff, then on to the fortress. Darkness was falling.

Chapter Twenty-six

The redcoats were hardly redcoats at all. Most of them did not look much like warriors. But they were strong and very determined. Two-feathers was impressed with their energy. He watched them unload the heavy fire-weapons from their ships and drag them across the beach and into the woods. There was something almost bear-like about them — slow and lumbering for the most part, then suddenly quick and cunning. He saw one particular element in them that distinguished them from the bluecoats right away: they were sharply focused on their objective. This element brought them together into a collective energy, and the energy made them dangerous. As he watched them force the heavy weapons across the difficult sand, over rocks and tree stumps and depressions in the land, he knew the bluecoats were in trouble. He had never seen this kind of determination among their people.

He watched until he had all the information he needed, then crossed the swamp to the fortress. But he quickly realized by the frenzied activity inside that the bluecoats already knew of their invaders. There was no need for him to warn them. Now was a time to rest. In the morning the redcoats would waste no time approaching the swamp. He wanted to be rested and ready for what he had been preparing for all summer and fall — to maintain an invisible presence in the field of battle.

In the morning, just as he had expected, the redcoats reconnoitered the swamp, without approaching the fortress. Two-feathers watched as a few quick-footed soldiers ran from bush to tree near the sparsely treed edge of the swamp. He knew it would take them several days to bring their heavy fire weapons to the swamp, so difficult was it to move them. The more he watched them the more certain he felt the bluecoats were going to suffer a terrible destruction.

In the afternoon he saw a contingent of bluecoats come out of the fortress and step onto the swamp. It was a rather small group. He wondered why they did not come out in force right away and attack the redcoats before they had time to entrench their position. And then he saw his father at the head of the contingent and Two-feathers was pleased. It was the first time he had ever felt any connection to his father. Here, now, they were on the same battlefield. Not only that, but in his father's face he no longer saw the look of a defeated man. Now he saw a warrior's scowl and a warrior's courage. Two-feathers was thrilled. For a moment he thought he might come up onto the field himself and go into battle alongside his father. But his father would not know who he was, nor likely believe him if he tried to explain, which would have been nearly impossible anyway. Besides, the bluecoats were already marching towards their enemy. There was no time for conversation.

Beneath the ground the bluecoats trod, Two-feathers kept pace with them as well as he could, until his tunnel system ended and he could go no further. Crouched inside one of his subterranean lookouts, he watched as a line of redcoats formed at the tree line, then moved forward to meet the advancing bluecoats.

It was a strange battle to witness. Neither side moved quickly. Everything took place slowly, with similar movements on both sides, as if there were some agreement between them as to how they would kill each other. Two-feathers watched his father especially, noting that every action of his was made with certainty and conviction, without a trace of fear or doubt. He felt proud.

The bluecoats fired their weapons first. The redcoats did not bother to take cover. What kind of fighting was this? Why would they stand open in front of each other's weapons? Now he knew that his father would have to leave himself open to their weapons because they had done so to his. Anything else would be dishonourable. Peering intensely through the lookout hole, never blinking, Two-feathers watched as smoke rose above the redcoats' weapons and his father fell to the ground.

The sight of it tore his heart. Pain gushed into it until it throbbed. He had no idea why he should feel this way. The warrior who was his father was a stranger to him. And yet, in the moment of his battle and death, Two-feathers felt as if they had become one. For one brief moment he carried knowledge of his father, and then he was gone.

Both sides continued to shoot each other for a while, but the redcoats soon took the advantage, as Two-feathers knew they would, and the bluecoats lost courage and ran back behind their walls.

Darkness fell. No one came to take the fallen bluecoats from the field. One young bluecoat stayed behind, ran to Two-feathers' father to check if he was dead, then ran back to the fortress when the redcoats shot at him. The bluecoats on the field died where they fell. Two-feathers did not think much of this sort of fighting. He could not see the sense in it. But he was proud of his father, and he would now treat him with the honour and respect that he deserved and that the spirits expected. It would be a privilege for Two-feathers to do this.

Racing back to his den, he began to construct a stretcher with which to carry his father's body away. Working feverishly hard, he wove a bed of reeds and branches between two poles and fastened bear-leather strips for tying the body down. In the darkness of night he crossed to the field where the body lay, pulled it onto the stretcher, tied it securely and dragged it away. He went across the swamp towards the woods. It was very hard work but he was glad to be doing it. Once he reached the shelter of the woods he took periodic rests. He followed a route he had taken many times before for hunting. He pulled the body all through the night and into the next day, resting only when he had to. He pulled it until he reached a gully by a river on the far side of a hill. There he constructed a teepee and a funeral pyre, all the while chanting prayers to the spirits. It would be the most important ceremony of his life, the burning of his father's body.

When the pyre was ready, Two-feathers lit the wood beneath it. The fire grew slowly because the wood was wet. It didn't matter. Eventually the flames would grow hot enough to consume everything within their grasp. As the smoke rose into the night sky he sat in front of his teepee and prayed. It was a bittersweet feeling watching the sparks float into the sky like fireflies. No longer did he have a parent living on this earth. His search was over. His childhood hopes of uniting with his father were over. But the unknowing was over too. Now there was just himself. It was now that he felt fully a man. Life was about acceptance. He felt this more than ever. Sometimes he would get what he wanted, and sometimes he wouldn't. His happiness, as his mother's spirit had told him, was in his acceptance of what did come. Neither should he despair when things were difficult, nor grow too confident when they were easy. Because they would change. Always, there would be change.

The fire burned through the night. In the morning he gathered the bones and carried them into the ice-filled river, laid them down and surrounded them with heavy stones. Then he returned to the teepee, constructed a bed of spruce boughs and went to sleep.

When night came once again he returned to the swamp. A quick investigation revealed that the redcoats had moved their cannon a little closer. The bluecoats were staying inside their walls, trusting in its fortifications. Two-feathers would go to the girl of the rainbow now and insist she leave with him. She was no longer safe.

Chapter Twenty-seven

My wound was not serious. The biggest threat was infection, and so the wound had to be cleaned thoroughly. I pulled a piece of shot out of my foot myself. Celestine helped me with the smaller pieces. I stared at my mother's pendant as she attended to my foot. It was more painful now because the skin had swollen. But Celestine was very careful and a lot gentler than any of the soldiers would have been – perhaps better than the surgeon would have. She cried the whole time. She cried for me losing my father. Losing her mother was the worst thing that had ever happened to her, she said. I felt that I ought to have cried too, but I couldn't really, maybe because she was crying so much.

But I was still in shock. Watching my father fall didn't seem real. Looking into his eyes and seeing him die didn't seem real. Nothing seemed real. But it was. I didn't feel that I loved my father and didn't feel that I didn't. I didn't know what I felt. I needed time to think about it. We had never formed a bond. He had always been disappointed in me. But now that he was gone, his disappointment didn't seem to matter anymore. I felt sorry for him dying like that, even though I knew it was the kind of death he had wanted. He had said so, many times. But I was sorry he was gone and that we would never have the chance to form a better relationship. Now it was too late. And I was sorry for my mother. I did not want to bring her this news. I would have to carry it for such a long time before I could give it to her, because I could not seem to bring myself to write it out for her in a letter.

Celestine sobbed as she pulled the tiny fragments from my foot, apologizing every time I winced. She cried enough for both of us.

"My father says that ships are on their way from France with reinforcements," she said between sobs. "Do you think they'll arrive in time?"

"Certainly. Besides, there is nothing the English can do. This is the strongest fortification in the New World."

I didn't really believe that, but I wanted her to feel better.

"I know. It's just that … soldiers have died already. I just wish everybody would stay inside now until the reinforcements come and chase the enemy away."

"Well, I think that is the plan."

"I know. That's what father says."

She was distressed. I sensed she was thinking of something else, or someone else. Finally, it came out. "Jacques?"

"Yes?"

"Do you believe the Natives have souls?"

"Of course they do. Just the same as us."

"Even if they don't believe the same things?"

"*We* don't all believe the same things."

"That's true. The other day I heard a man say that the English are evil. Do you think they are?"

"Not at all. I have friends who are English. And they are wonderful. You would really like them."

"Even when they killed your father?"

"My father chose to die like that."

"What do you mean? That's mad! Your father never chose to die."

"No, but he chose to fight. He stood up in front of their muskets and waited for them to shoot him. I saw it with my own eyes."

She looked at me with horror. "Your father was a hero. He gave his life trying to protect us."

"I know. It's just that he believed in fighting. He was proud to die like that."

Celestine dropped her head and continued cleaning my wound and sobbing. I didn't want to talk about it anymore. I could feel the divide between us and I was in no mood to try to bridge it. "Thank you for cleaning my wound."

"You're welcome," she said tearfully. "Could you please see my father before you leave? He wants to talk with you."

"Yes. Of course."

I limped downstairs. M. Anglaise was wearing an expression of profound sympathy.

"Your father was a courageous man, Jacques. We are forever in his debt."

"Yes, sir."

"He died for what he believed in. But it is our loss."

"Yes, sir."

He was about to say something else, then changed his mind.

"Jacques. We outnumber the English. They are a bunch of farmers and fishermen, just as I had predicted. They also have a naval contingent. And they appear to have it in their minds to haul their cannon across the swamp and lay siege to the fortress."

"Yes, sir."

"It is a fool's plan, I think. Nevertheless, should they ever get their cannon within striking range of the fortress we will suffer much loss of life."

I nodded.

"Now, we are expecting ships from France any day, with more soldiers and supplies. When they arrive, we will make a concerted attack against this invasion and send them fleeing back to their farms and villages in New England."

"Of course we will, sir."

"All the same, Jacques, I want to share a private word with you."

He stepped closer to me and softened his voice as if there were someone else listening. There wasn't.

"Should the winds of fortune favour the English and they manage to miraculously defeat us ..."

"But ..."

"No. Hear me out."

"Yes, sir."

"Should they defeat us here in this dismal, forsaken place, then, by the etiquette of war they will promptly return me and my family to France. Heaven help the common people of this town, but they will escort me and my family in a fashion befitting my station in society. Do you understand?"

"Yes, sir."

"Good. I want you to understand that I hereby consider you as my own son. Is this agreeable to you?"

I was speechless. He reached over and put his hand on my shoulder. "Do you find this arrangement acceptable, Jacques?"

"I ... I don't know what to say, sir."

"Then say yes, Jacques. Say yes."

"Yes, sir."

"Good. We needn't speak of it again. Should the unthinkable occur, I will inform the invading officers who the members of my family are."

"Thank you, sir."

"No. Thank *you*, Jacques. Thank you and your father from the bottom of my heart."

M. Anglaise turned towards the window. I started to go.

"Jacques?"

"Sir?"

"You are hereby relieved of your military duties."

"Are you certain, sir? We are under attack."

"More than certain, Jacques. Louisbourg's fate will not rest upon the shoulders of one soldier more or less. France, on the other hand, is in desperate need of enlightened men. Nurse your wounds, Jacques, in your foot and in your heart."

"Yes, sir."

Chapter Twenty-eight

They worked with the strength and persistence of ants but they did not always work harmoniously. Even from a distance Two-feathers witnessed arguments between them. It was always an argument between a warrior dressed in red and those who were not. The arguments appeared to concern the movement and placement of their fire weapons. They struggled so hard he sometimes wondered if they would give up trying to cross the swamp and try another tactic.

He had also seen redcoats disappear into the woods where he did his hunting. He saw bluecoats enter the same woods from the other side and heard the distant crackle of their weapons. Now he would have to use extra caution entering the woods and travel further away for hunting. In fact, everything had changed with the coming of the redcoats and he had not been able to visit the girl of the rainbow since. The bluecoats were guarding their village like never before. They kept constant watch with many soldiers at every wall. And though he was actually allied with the bluecoats, they did not know him and would not trust him if he appeared just when the redcoats did. He would have to find another way in.

He sat in his den and considered what to do. The redcoats were advancing across the swamp very slowly. His tunnel system occupied just one section of the swamp, closer to the fortress.

Eventually the redcoats would reach it and, with the weight of their weapons, would likely fall through the tunnels. He would have to leave. He had mixed feelings about that. On one hand he was tired of the swamp and anxious to live in the woods again. On the other hand he had invested so much time and effort constructing his tunnel system it seemed a shame to leave it. It was the most work he had ever done and he was proud of it. As it turned out, things were decided for him.

He had been checking his food stores, much depleted over the winter, when he sensed movement outside the tunnel. Hurrying to one of his lookouts he spied a large warrior cautiously scouting the ground for a suitable path for the fire-weapons. Two-feathers watched closely as the soldier stepped right above one of the dens. Suddenly, the soldier fell through. With a yell he disappeared into the ground. Two-feathers heard the man's shouts echo faintly inside the tunnel. Rushing outside he watched him climb out of the hole and pick himself up. As he turned, he saw Two-feathers and looked frightened. He reached for his musket. Two-feathers fitted an arrow to his bow. As the soldier raised his weapon and took aim, Two-feathers let the arrow fly and shot him in the arm. The soldier dropped his musket and pulled the arrow from his arm with a holler. He reached for his musket once again but Two-feathers had already fitted another arrow and was aiming for the man's heart. The soldier saw this and froze. Two-feathers hesitated. He did not want to take the life of this man. His mind drifted back to standing with his chief in the woods and asking him if it was harder to shoot a man than an animal. His chief had answered that when the reason was sufficient, the shooting was the same. Two-feathers searched his heart. There did not seem sufficient reason. Then he searched his mind and there he found an answer: "This is not my war."

Two-feathers lowered his bow. The soldier stared for a second, disbelieving, then ran away as fast as he could.

It was time to go. Two-feathers gathered up his bearskin, his necklace, tools and weapons, tied them onto his back and left the swamp. As he entered the forest he said goodbye to the spirits of the muskrat and owl and thanked them for their help.

After a day's journey, he chose a secluded spot and constructed a teepee. He hunted, made a fire, and chanted prayers while his food was roasting. It occurred to him that he might just keep going. The woods were so appealing, why go back? The bluecoats' village had become a dangerous place now for everyone. And, as he had just realized, this was not his war. His father was gone. His mother was at peace. He had accomplished what he had come to do.

But there was the girl of the rainbow and there were the métis children. As he poked at the fire with a stick he imagined redcoats running around inside the walls attacking everyone and setting the village on fire. It was not his war, this was true, but he was in love with the girl of the rainbow. He must rescue her. And the children were his people. He had promised to feed them. He had to go back.

He prepared a basket of food, strapped it to his back and travelled through the night. He approached the fortress from the water. With the walls so heavily guarded now, the rocky shoreline was the best way to get in. The wall by the water, with its long, silent fire-weapons jutting out every fifty paces or so, was low enough for him to climb over wherever he wished, though there were no hidden shelters, only the weapons. He went from one weapon to the next in the heavy fog of morning, then made a dash for the long warehouse where the children were hiding. He found them in their corner, lying close together in their blankets and old coats. There were five of them. The youngest was barely old enough to hold a bow, the oldest, at an age where she ought to know how to skin a deer.

The children gobbled the food and looked for more. Two-feathers asked were they not getting any food elsewhere? No, they said, not now. They were too afraid to go outside. Why? he asked. Because there was a terrible enemy coming. They had heard people talking. The terrible enemy would do horrible things to them. They would cut their heads off and burn them alive. This was not true, Two-feathers said, though they were smart to stay inside for now. There was an enemy, this was true, but they were not so different from the bluecoats. He did not believe they would hurt children. But stay inside, he told them. Tomorrow he would bring them more food. But would he protect them? they asked. Would he come and rescue them if the enemy came?

Two-feathers looked at the frightened faces of the children. Then he thought of the girl of the rainbow. He didn't know how he could save them both. Would he save them? they asked again. He didn't answer. He thought for a moment to ask the spirits, but hesitated. He didn't know why he hesitated. Was he afraid of their answer? No. It wasn't that. It was because he knew the answer already. He shouldn't bother the spirits with questions for which he already knew the answer.

Yes, he said with a heavy sigh. Yes, he would save them. Don't forget, the children said as they wrapped up in their blankets and coats. He wouldn't forget, he said. Did he promise? they asked. Yes, he answered. He promised.

In his dream that night Two-feathers heard the voice of his mother in the wind. "You are more than a warrior now," she said.

"I am a warrior," Two-feathers insisted.

"You are tasting the bittersweetness of sacrifice," said his mother. "You are more than a warrior now."

Two-feathers felt the wind brush against him, pick him up and carry him through the air as if he were a leaf. "I am a warrior," he repeated.

"My son," said his mother.

Chapter Twenty-nine

If you believed as my father had then you would have thought cannon one of the greatest inventions ever conceived. He regarded them with a respect I never knew him to hold for any person, except perhaps a few other engineers and, of course, the King. That a cannon could hurl a heavy ball through the air for miles, knock a hole in a ship and send it to the bottom of the sea was a fact that caused him no end of pleasure. Once a cannonball was in the air there was no force on earth that could stop it. Heaven help whatever lay in its way.

I didn't know much about them myself, but, like everyone else in the fortress lying in their path, I learned fast. As it turned out, cannon were a pretty crude weapon. They were ridiculously inaccurate to begin with. This was why ships had to get so close to each other in a naval battle. Otherwise, most of their cannonballs would simply drop to the ocean floor.

In the case of shooting into a fortress it was hard for them to know if they were causing any damage. Unlike a ship, which would sink once it received a few holes, the English wouldn't know if their cannonballs were actually hitting anything or just landing on the ground, whereby we could pick them up and use them ourselves. Although, since we didn't have any cannon pointing towards the swamp, we couldn't shoot them back. But we could stockpile them in case the enemy should ever sail into our harbour.

The English had other options, though, which were more dangerous. Firstly, they could heat up the cannonballs in fires until they were red hot, then drop them into their cannon and shoot them into the fortress. If the balls landed on a roof or got stuck in a wall they would start a fire.

And there was something worse. Mortar shells were heavier than regular cannonballs and were shot out of special, short-barrelled cannon. Inside a mortar shell was a stock of gunpowder that exploded when it hit something, causing the ball to burst apart in hundreds of pieces and start fires. The English could tell where a mortar shell had landed and if it had caused much damage. When they first arrived, their cannon were lying on the far side of the swamp and were not close enough to cause us any concern. But as the weeks progressed and they grew closer to the fortress, everything changed dramatically.

I spent all my time with my newly adopted family now, partly because we played music to take our minds off the war, and partly because M. Anglaise invited me to stay in his sitting rooms. In fact, he often asked me to stay around even when the officers came to consult with M. Duchambon. And M. Duchambon would ask my opinions on things too, even though, like M. Anglaise, I didn't have a military mind. I began to feel sorry for M. Duchambon then because he was surrounded by officers waiting upon his command in the middle of a military disaster and never really seemed to know what to do at any given moment. I think he was uncomfortable making decisions when people were dying.

During the early stages of the conflict we wondered which would happen first: would the English get their cannon across the swamp, or would ships arrive from France? If we had known then that the ships were never coming in the first place, we would have saved a lot of time wondering and hoping. Secretly, I think M. Anglaise suspected as much. In front of M. Duchambon and the officers he spoke of how valuable Louisbourg was to France. But when they left the room he admitted to me that he had met the King on more than one occasion, and he assured me that the King would have traded the Fortress of Louisbourg and all of its inhabitants in a game of cards. "How right Plato was, Jacques, and even our flamboyant Voltaire – monarchy is a most inequitable thing. How vain the fate of the many should rest upon the whims of the one."

I felt sorry for Celestine. She seemed to carry more fear of the English than anyone else, especially now that my father had been killed. It had also been a while since she had shared any roasted food with me and I imagined she worried about *him* too, even though we never talked about that. Ever since the English had arrived, the fortress was too heavily guarded for even a ghost to invade. I wondered where he was now and what he was up to. Celestine must also have been wondering what had become of him.

The first cannonballs landed in the field outside the walls. Through the telescope glass I saw the English labouring like to move their cannon closer. I really couldn't fathom their motivation.

"Do they hate the French so much, sir?" I asked M. Anglaise.

"Oh, no, I don't think so. They hate Catholicism, no doubt. But the New Englanders have been coming up here to trade with us for years. They generally have a good time in the town, make a fair trade and go home. I know some of them by name."

"But … why would they try so hard now, sir? They seem to have a fire in them our soldiers lack."

"Indeed," said M. Anglaise, as he squinted to look through the telescope glass. "I suppose we have our King to thank for that. He started it by declaring war."

"Yes, sir. "

"Declaring war on England is declaring war on the colonists. I suppose they don't take too kindly to that. They're willing to fight and die for their land. You and I and the majority of the soldiers in this fortress are not willing to die for this place, I dare say. Why would we give our lives for such a forsaken place?"

"My father did, sir."

He pulled the glass from his eye, stood up straight and looked at me remorsefully. "He did, Jacques. He did indeed."

I didn't know why I'd said that. It just jumped out of me. With each passing day it seemed more ridiculous to me that my father had died the way he did. What had he accomplished by it? What had he proved? I had no answer for that. I had no clear feelings about it at all and I sensed it would be a long time before I did.

After a few more days the cannonballs began to reach the moat. The water splashed high into the air and rained down inside the walls. Then, finally, came the dull concussion of metal hitting stone. It was surprisingly destructive to the walls. A single hit could destroy several large stones and cause a crack right down the wall. If the walls had not been as thick as they were, they would have crumbled immediately.

Our soldiers worked hard to make wooden repairs to the walls. This at least held the walls up, behind which they could take cover and shoot the enemy if it dared to advance within musket range. They also tried to reposition our smaller cannon to shoot at the swamp. But with no structure to shoot at, and the enemy constantly moving around, the little cannon offered little help. And we were almost out of gunpowder. It was one of the supplies we were waiting for so anxiously from France.

Each day the cannonballs landed further into the interior of the fortress. Most of the houses lay down the hill, away from the swamp. But the Governor's residence began to take hits. M. Anglaise was urged to change residence immediately but he refused, displaying a surprising amount of courage for a man without a fighting sensibility. Personally I would have preferred us to move, but I stayed and kept company with Celestine.

Chapter Thirty

Coming from the woods at night, Two-feathers saw a flash of light in the swamp, heard a roar, then saw a burst of fire inside the bluecoats' village. Flames shot up into the nighttime sky. People were screaming. It was more than fear; it was the sound of horror. People were dying. He thought of the girl of the rainbow. He must help her. He thought of the children too and remembered his promise.

With the pack of food on his back he ran all the way to the beach and entered from the water near the main gate. There were more explosions. People were running everywhere, screaming. Not bothering to hide, he ran to the warehouse where the children were anxiously waiting for him. It had been more than two days since his last visit. Handing the food to them he asked them if they were all right. They were frightened, they said. There were such loud noises and shouting and screaming. He looked at their frightened faces and told them not to worry. He had to look for someone else but would come back for them. He promised. If the building were to catch on fire, he said, run out the door and down to the water. Hide in the rocks there and wait for him. He would come back and take them away. The children nodded their heads and gobbled up the food. Two-feathers went out the door.

Several houses were on fire. Running up the street towards the leader's house he saw it engulfed in flames. Was he too late? He ran into the courtyard. No one was guarding the gate. All of the soldiers were too busy trying to put out fires or were up on the walls firing their muskets. Then, he saw the girl of the rainbow. She was running towards him with something in her arms. She was being chased by a redcoat! Two-feathers fitted an arrow to his bow. There was so much smoke everywhere it was difficult to see. Afraid to shoot her, he stepped to the side. Just then, the redcoat lunged towards her. Two-feathers let his arrow fly. At that second there was a deafening noise and he was knocked to the ground.

He lay still for a long time, unable to get up. Someone took hold of him and tried to move him. It was the redcoat! Two-feathers asked the spirits if he was dead. No, they said. Was he going to die? No. Why couldn't he get up then? He could get up, they said. His ears were ringing. He raised his head slowly and tried to look around. Everything was covered with smoke. He saw the redcoat running away. There was shouting and more explosions, but everything sounded so far away, so strangely far away. He dropped his head again. He was so tired.

He did not know how long he lay there, but when he was finally able to rise to his knees, the smoke had lifted. There were explosions further away. He looked for the girl of the rainbow, but she was gone. He looked around the courtyard, hardly recognizing it. The walls were broken apart. Everything was in flames. Blue-coats were running frantically here and there.

Getting to his feet he staggered over to the leader's house. It was completely wrapped in flames and the heat was intense. Anyone inside would be dead now. The girl of the rainbow must have escaped. There was no sign of the redcoat. Two-feathers was confused. He was sure his arrow had hit its mark. His head was throbbing and his ears ringing. Then he thought of the children and started down the hill towards them.

He staggered through the leader's gate, turned towards the warehouse and saw it in flames. He started to run, but it made his head ache unbearably. Reaching the front door, he discovered a wall of flames. He could not go inside. The children must have escaped to the water, he thought. Otherwise they were dead. Praying to the spirits that he would find the children amongst the rocks at the beach, he hurried down to the water. The children were there.

They cried when they saw him. Two-feathers told them that everything was going to be all right now; he would look after them. But they continued to cry and were trying to tell him something. He realized then that there were only four of them. One, a boy of seven or eight years, was missing. Where was he? Two-feathers asked. Sobbing, they told him that the boy had gone back inside the warehouse for something and never came out. Two-feathers dropped his head. All right, he said. Wait here. He would find him and come back. The children nodded and crouched back down among the rocks.

He ran back to the burning warehouse and stared at the door. It was a wall of flames, but the warehouse was deep. He doubted the entire space was filled with fire. Still, he felt afraid. If he were wrong, he would burn to death. If he didn't go, the boy would burn to death. He took a deep breath and charged through the flames. As he had guessed, there were spaces inside that were not burning, but the air was intensely hot and it was impossible to breathe. He raced over to the corner where the children had been hiding. There, curled up on the ground, with a black case in his arms, was the boy. He had gone to sleep in the smoke, but Two-feathers could tell he was still alive. He picked him up, but the boy's hands were so tightly clasped around the handle of the black case that he lifted that with him. As the rafters began to fall around them, Two-feathers ran through the wall of flames again and carried the boy down to the beach. There, in the cold seawater the boy revived, coughing violently to chase the smoke from his lungs.

Two-feathers led the children from the fortress and into the woods. The oldest carried the youngest on her back. Two-feathers carried the boy who had been in the fire. Someone else carried his case. It was for this case the boy had risked his life, said the children. Two-feathers asked them what was in it but didn't understand when they told him. Never mind, they said, their brother would show him later.

The children were tired but Two-feathers insisted they travel through the rest of the night until they reached a place that was safe from the redcoats. There they would rest for a day and he would hunt for them. After they had rested and eaten they would travel many days from the sea, to a place where the redcoats and bluecoats never go. There they would make a camp where they would stay for a long time. They would hunt and fish and make prayers to the spirits. Who were the spirits? the children asked. Would he tell them? Yes, said Two-feathers, he would tell them everything.

Chapter Thirty-one

It was a night of terror. The English had tricked us into a state of calm by not shooting their cannon in the day. Little did we know it was because they were preparing for a nighttime mortar assault.

We were standing in the Governor's room, Celestine, her father and myself, discussing the fact that people were starving in the fortress. M. Duchambon was outside with the officers. Many townspeople, including some soldiers, had fled the fortress and given themselves up to the enemy already. Strategically this was a disaster because the deserters could tell the English our state of affairs, in particular that we were more or less out of gunpowder and praying for ships to arrive from France. Pressure for the acting Governor to surrender was enormous, and we all knew it was inevitable. The longer he held out, the more people would die, and that weighed heavily on his conscience, said M. Anglaise. And yet, M. Duchambon held on.

"What happens here, Jacques," M. Anglaise said to me as if he were apologizing on M. Duchambon's behalf, "concerns far more than just our particular selves. This is the nature of diplomacy, do you see?"

"Yes, sir."

"When we return to France …"

He was in mid sentence when a mortar shell struck the residence. We ran down the stairs and rushed out the door to see. Flames were coming out of the building down on the far side. A woman was screaming hysterically in the distance.

"Jacques!" said M. Anglaise. "Quick! Help me with my papers!"

"Yes, sir."

"You're not going back in!" said Celestine, glaring at her father. He stared at her with a look of despair and regret, and I knew it was because he wished he had never taken her to this place. He didn't answer her, he just ran back inside.

"We have to get out of here!" she said tearfully.

"I know," I said. "We will."

I ran in after M. Anglaise. There were more mortar crashes and more screaming. I looked behind me for Celestine but she had not followed us in. M. Anglaise rifled through some papers quickly but was distracted with too many thoughts at once. Suddenly he reached for one of his coats, a bright red one, and flung it at me. "Put it on, Jacques. They will know you are my son. Where is Celestine?"

"Waiting outside, sir."

I pulled the jacket on.

"Here!" he said. "Put these in the pockets."

He handed me a thick pile of papers. I dropped them into the front pocket where they hung heavily. Another mortar struck the residence. All of the windows shattered. There was a soft humming sound and a sharp crackling. The fire was spreading quickly.

"Please, Jacques. Go out and stay with Celestine now. I will be right out."

I stood for a moment, unsure whether or not to go.

"Go!" he commanded.

"Yes, sir."

I ran out the door and found Celestine where we had left her, only now she was sobbing uncontrollably like a child. I embraced her. "It will be okay," I said, though I hardly believed it myself.

Mortar shells went over our heads with a strange hissing sound. The English were now firing higher, aiming into the town in an attempt to terrorize the people. The fire in the Governor's residence was rising high into the sky.

"My father!" Celestine cried. "Where is my father?"

"He's coming. I promise you. He's coming."

Truly, I did not know if he was. Together we stood and stared at the door. There was another explosion. I almost dashed in to look for him. Suddenly, we saw him appear with an armload of papers. He ran with his head down.

"Quick! Come!" he said. "Follow me!"

I held Celestine's arm as we followed M. Anglaise along the courtyard, taking care to step around burning cinders on the grass. Then, Celestine broke free of my grasp and yelled, "I have to get something!"

"What?" I said. "No! There's nothing to get!"

"I have to get something!" she yelled, and ran back to the burning entrance. I turned to see what M. Anglaise would do but he had not heard her and had not stopped. I tried to call him back but he couldn't hear me. So I turned and ran back after her. When I saw her disappear inside the door I truly thought she was going to die. What on earth could have been so valuable that she would run back into a burning building for it?

"Celestine!" I yelled at the top of my lungs. "Celestine!"

I stood at the doorway but did not go in. "Celestine! Are you mad?!"

I should have gone in after her, but I didn't. Something – fear, I suppose – kept me from crossing the threshold into the flames that were leaping up from the floor and coming through the walls. The heat was unbearable just standing at the doorway. I stood there, fixed to my spot and thought: should I go in? Should I go in? But I never did.

Then I saw her. She came awkwardly down the stairs carrying something over her head. It was the violoncello. Outside, we started to run again. It was so chaotic. I saw people racing back and forth, and then, a mortar shell came over the wall and was about to hit the residence beside us. "Celestine!" I yelled, and lunged towards her with all my might. I felt something strike me in my chest, knocking the wind out of me. Then the mortar exploded and I lost sight of everything.

When the smoke cleared I found myself sitting on the ground. My face was burning and my ears were ringing. Reaching up with my hand I was shocked to discover an arrow lodged in my chest. I couldn't believe it. Feeling inside my clothes I found that the arrow had not reached my skin. It was embedded in M. Anglaise's papers. Getting to my feet I found Celestine on the ground not far away. She was stunned but able to rise. As we staggered forward I saw out of the corner of my eye someone, a Native, lying on the ground. I was pretty sure it was my ghost.

"Hurry!" I yelled to Celestine. "Catch up with your father. I will bring the violoncello."

I ran over to the Native and tried to raise him but he was too heavy for me and I was too weak. At least I could see that he was alive and that he was real, not a ghost at all. I wished I could have helped him, but Celestine was screaming for me to come.

"Good luck, my friend!" I said to him, squeezed his hand and ran away.

———

The acting Governor surrendered after the night of terror. There were few people willing to stay in the fortress any longer, especially as there were no signs of ships coming from France. The English had created an effective blockade, and so even if ships did arrive from France they would not have been able to enter the harbour.

M. Duchambon held out as long as he felt was diplomatically necessary. Then we were put on board the English navy's finest ship,
in all manner of comfort, and carried back to France, via England.

———

It was a surprisingly pleasant voyage. The ship cut through choppy
waves as it cleared the harbour and headed northeast into the Atlantic. Strong winds carried us in an arc all the way to England.
It was a large ship with fine windows and comfortable berths. M.
Anglaise, Celestine and myself were given cabins. We would be
taken to England first, and from there given in exchange for English nobility held in France. I found the ship very comfortable, the
food decent enough and the company of the captain, in particular,
quite agreeable. He was well educated, fluent in the French language, highly opinionated and fond of the music of Handel.

M. Anglaise also found our accommodation and treatment
very acceptable. He had expected nothing less. Celestine, on the
other hand, was in a dark mood the entire first week. She seemed
to resent that her father and I were enjoying the Captain's company so much.

"How can you *talk* to him so?" she asked bitterly.

I shrugged my shoulders. "Why not?"

"Because they are evil," she said under her breath. "They killed
our people. They killed your father for Heaven's sake! I hate the
English!"

I didn't know what to say. I knew there were good and bad
people on both sides. I believed that the person most responsible
for the death of the people at Louisburg was the one who had
started it all in the first place – the King.

But I was sorry my father had died. I wished I didn't have to
bring this news home to my mother. Something else was start-
ing to bother me too, though I sensed this was just the beginning
of coming to grips with my father's death. I realized that I had
never played the violoncello for him. He had always been away or
too busy. Now, I would never have the chance. I couldn't help but

wonder: if he had heard me play, would it have made any difference? Would it have changed anything? Would he have recognized in my love for music something akin to his love for weapons and war? Perhaps. Perhaps not. But the thought haunted me because now, I would never know. Death was final.

I had been deeply impressed by his courage in battle. I wished I could have told him that. It was something he had that I didn't have. We might have had a conversation about it, I thought. And then I wondered about his body. The soldiers' bodies had been left on the field. M. Anglaise told me that the English would bury them. It was part of the etiquette of war. The captain assured me this was true. That helped, although not being there to witness it bothered me. I felt I should have been there when my father's bones were laid in the ground.

There were so many other things I would have liked to discuss with him. Would he have liked that? Would he have respected me when I was older? I wished I knew. People have said that we carry regret not for what we have done, but for what we have failed to do. I never shed a tear on the day my father died. Now, on our way back home, in the privacy of my own cabin, my tears began to fall. But they were not tears for all that had happened. They were tears for what might have and now never could.

After a week at sea, Celestine's mood began to lift. We brought out the violoncello when the captain learned that we could play. The bridge had been destroyed on our flight from the residence so he had the ship's carpenter fashion a new one. The irony of this Atlantic crossing, compared with my first one, was not lost on me as I rosined up the bow and entertained our host with the music of Bach and Handel. After much coaxing, Celestine also agreed to play, to her father's great pleasure. I was surprised to see that she had taken off my mother's pendant and was wearing a necklace made of a bear claw, wild but pretty. As I passed the violoncello to her she put something into my hand and whispered, "I think this belongs to you more than me."

In my hand I found my mother's pendant. I stared pleadingly into Celestine's eyes, begging to know how she knew that. How could she know? Had she known all along? She dropped her eyes and turned her face away. "Thank you," I whispered. She nodded without looking at me.

"Such exquisite playing on my ship this evening," said the captain. Then, eyeing the bear-claw necklace, he said, "What a fine piece of Native jewellery."

He turned to me. "Tell me, Jacques. You have spent a whole year in the New World. Would you describe it as a savage place?"

I thought about it. "I suppose so, sir, though the worst savagery I have witnessed here is the savagery of war, and I do believe that we brought it with us."

"Indeed."

As Celestine began to play, I thought of my ghost. I wondered where he was now. What was he thinking about? Had he seen us leave? Did he know we would never come back? Had he chance to speak with Celestine before the end? How I wished I knew. And would I ever see him again? No. I knew I wouldn't. I was going home and I would never come back.

Epilogue

The deer stood alone in the clearing, a buck with an imposing set of antlers. He sniffed the air, suspicious of something.
Two-feathers reached for an arrow. Behind him, five little heads
crouched. Having practised invisibility in the fortress, they were
learning invisibility in the woods.

"Now," whispered Two-feathers, "we apologize to the deer
and thank him for giving us his life."

The children nodded in agreement. Then one of them said,
"But he hasn't given us his life yet. Why are we thanking him for
it already?"

"Because he is going to," whispered Two-feathers.

"How do you know?" asked the child.

"Because I am going to shoot him now."

But when Two-feathers looked up, the buck was gone. It took
two more hours to track him again. This time the children agreed
not to say anything but to make their prayers silently in their
heads. As they furrowed their brows and concentrated hard, Two-
feathers fitted his arrow and let it fly. The arrow pierced the front
left flank of the buck and he dropped to his knees. A second arrow
immediately followed and brought the buck down. Two-feathers
shot a third into the neck. Too many times he had seen a fallen
deer rise to its feet and bolt. Running over, he stabbed the heart to
make certain the suffering was over. Then he dropped his head in
gratitude. The children came and admired the deer.

"He is so beautiful."

"It is sad that he had to die."

"It is not sad," said Two-feathers. "We all die. Then we live as
spirits. Then we are always happy. So it is not sad to die."

"Tell us more about the spirits," said the children.

"Tonight, while we eat our supper I will begin to tell you
about them."

He hung the buck from a tree and let the children watch as he skinned it. The hide, he explained, would make very comfortable clothing for the fall. They would all need some. He also took the antlers and pieces of bone for making needles and various other tools. He cut as much meat as he felt they could eat, and some to carry, then burned the carcass in a fire, intending to place the bones in the river the next morning. The children watched everything with fascination.

When they returned to their teepee it was dark. The children huddled together in the bearskin as Two-feathers began to roast their supper over the fire. The boy with the black case opened it and pulled out a smooth wooden instrument with strings. He also took out a stick tied with horsehair. Two-feathers watched curiously as the boy twisted one end of the stick and fitted the instrument between his chin and shoulder. He raised his arm and laid the stick across the strings. Tapping his foot three or four times, he slipped the stick back and forth and the instrument began to sing. Two-feathers stood up. He was amazed. This was the music he had heard trading parties and soldiers play in the woods. It was wonderful. On and on the boy played, with a skill that impressed Two-feathers greatly. The children smiled and sang along, and eventually they got up and danced.

"What is it called?" Two-feathers asked them.

"A fiddle," said the children.

"How do you play it?"

The boy handed the fiddle to Two-feathers and showed him how to hold it and how to draw the bow across the strings. But the sound he produced was weak and scratchy. The children laughed. Two-feathers smiled and handed the instrument back. "I will hunt," he said to the boy, "and you will play. Agreed?"

"Agreed," said the boy.

After they ate, the children sat around the fire and listened as Two-feathers explained how all of the animals and plants had spirits. Even the rivers had spirits, he said, and the wind and the rain. There were spirits everywhere, all of the time. They were always there and you could talk to them. But you had to learn to be very, very quiet if you wanted to hear them talking back. There were many things that he could teach them himself, such as how to hunt and cook, how to sew and fashion baskets and canoes, how to build shelters and survive in the winter. But there were many more things that only the spirits could teach them, and for that they would have to learn to listen, each in his or her own way.

The children listened carefully because Two-feathers only spoke when he had something interesting to say. But one question would always lead to another. There was one thing in particular the children wanted to know. The oldest put it into words.

"Two-feathers, if we are not French, and we are not Mi'kmaq, then who are we?"

Two-feathers took a stick out of the fire and pointed to two stars in the sky. "We are some of both," he said, "and we are neither." Then he pointed to a third star burning brightly. "We are something new."

The End

Acknowledgements

I have received so much support and good advice on the writing of this book from family and friends. In particular I want to acknowledge my mother, Ellen; my daughter, Julia; and sons, Peter and Thomas. I also want to mention Lydia Race, who has been such an enthusiastic reader of the story; and greatest friends, Chris, Natasha and Chiara, who put a smile on everything. I would like to acknowledge my friends, Diana, Maria and Sammy; Dale and Jake; Hugh; my dear Zaan; and my darling Leila (and Fritzi). Mike Hunter at CBU has given terrific guidance, and I am indebted to the sharp eye and critical pen of Kate Kennedy.

An Acadian-Mi'kmaw Background

Ten generations ago, my ancestor, Jean Roy du Laliberté, sailed from St. Malo, France, to the land that would eventually become Nova Scotia. At Cap-Sable, the most southwestern tip of the peninsula, he married Marie (Christine) Aubois (Dubois), a woman of Maliseet blood, or, as she is listed in the historical record, "Amérindienne." Their marriage was registered on the 3rd of March, 1706. They were no spring chickens; he was fifty-five and she was forty-one. In fact, Marie had borne nine children by then, though one of them had died. It was common for a marriage to be registered years after it actually took place. It was also common for a French soldier to take a wife from the Mi'kmaq, or neighboring Maliseet people. It gave them considerable advantage in the New World.

It is difficult to imagine any physical likeness to Jean or Marie after so many generations – the blood has been thinned by some fiercely individualistic Scottish and Irish farmers – yet the heritage is there; the name is there. If you go back a generation or two in family photos, you see Métis blood in the faces there.

It seems that the older we get the more interest we take in people who came before us – they walked the same soil, climbed the same hills, trekked through the same woods and stared at the ocean from the same beaches. Did they ever wonder about us, as we might wonder about those who will come after us? Perhaps they did from time to time, though they must have been preoccupied with the business of survival, and they must have been very tough because this was a rugged place before there were roads and railways, electricity and modern medicine. Now, we have the leisure to look back and study them, write about them, dramatize them – yet behind the dramas that we create are individuals who really stood here in this place and made a claim upon it. The longer one contemplates this, the more remarkable it becomes.

My mother's people were Scottish and Irish. Her paternal ancestors made the trip from Scotland in the 1780s aboard the

Hector, a rather small, fat, aged sailing ship that has been replicated and sits in the water as a museum in Pictou Harbour, Nova Scotia. My mother's people –staunch Catholics – settled in the Protestant community of Pictou, where they adopted the Protestant faith just long enough to get the wherewithal to move to Cape Breton, reclaiming their Catholicism and setting roots. My grandfather, Joe (Big Joe) MacDonald, heralds from Troy, Cape Breton.

In my research for this novel I came upon an interesting item in J. S. McLennan's celebrated book *Louisbourg: From its Foundations to its Fall*. Among the ships McLennan lists as having supported the 1745 siege of Louisbourg is the *Hector*. She was a much younger ship then. A generation after helping defeat the French and allies – my father's ancestors – she would carry my mother's people to the same land. This is exactly the kind of coincidental historical fact that tweaks my imagination. Come to think of it, there's probably a whole novel in that.

P.R.

About the Author

Philip Roy was born and raised in Antigonish, Nova Scotia. He studied music with Sister Rodriquez Steele and Professor James Hargreaves and aspired to a career as a pianist. After graduating from high school, he left Antigonish to work and travel. As a young man, he returned to the study of piano with Oriole Aitchison in Halifax, where he also began composing music. Af-

ter getting married, Philip moved to Ontario and devoted his time to raising his children, later returning to school and degrees in history at University of Waterloo and McMaster University. Master's degrees in hand, he moved to the island of Saipan in Micronesia, where he taught English and history in a high school for two years. Following that, he returned to Canada and settled for a time in Ontario, teaching piano.

The lure of his home province eventually brought Philip back to Nova Scotia, where he began writing young adult novels and stories for children. In 2008, his first novel, *Submarine Outlaw*, was published by Ronsdale Press of Vancouver. The fifth book in the series, *Outlaw in India*, will be released at the same time as *Blood Brothers in Louisbourg*. Philip currently lives in Halifax, where he continues to write novels and compose music.